The Wood Witch's Daughter

The Wood Witch's Daughter

Kate Seger

.

For All the Dreamers.

There is always hope. If only because it is the one thing we haven't figured out how to kill... yet.

The Wood Witch's Daughter

CONTENTS

PROLOGUE

"In the beginning there was one Realm, and one rule -- the Great Mother Xennia's. For eons there was peace between Elven and Mankind. Then came the Fae, with their Courts and their hierarchy, their precious bloodlines. They enslaved the gentle Elves and the frail Mortals.

The Elves, wielders of the most powerful magic, foresaw the bloodshed that lay ahead and created the Veil. When the Great War came, as they knew it would, they divided the Realm. On one side of the Veil, Onerth haven of the Mortals. On the other, the Ethereal Realms, a land of rampant magic ruled over by the tyrannical Fae Courts.

Two Courts stood with the Elves when they rose against the Courts: the Dreamers, who believed in the Elven goal of one peaceful realm, and the Sky Fae, ever their allies.

Resistance was futile, their defeat was written in blood on the walls.

The Wood Witch's Daughter

The Court of Dreams fell, their lineage and that of the Elves ended in one fell swoop. The Sky Fae avoided utter annihilation but paid a steep price. Only the Mortals, safe in Onerth were spared the yoke of the Fae coalition's fury.

This is the tale that the Courts of Shadow, Fire, Sea, and Earth would have you believe. But it is not the entire story. There is a prophecy that says that the Legion Queen will come to unite the three races of the land in harmony once again.

The time draws nigh when all must choose a side."

~The History of the Lost Folk
By Múirgan Vivane

CHAPTER 1

A BITTERSWEET MELODY

The high keening sound of a woman singing mingled with birdsong and the low drone of insects. Something that did not belong, altering the melody of the primordial Greenwood. Arianette Gracelilly lifted her head, listening. She rose, following the sound, moving deftly through the underbrush, darting between the broad trunks of white birch and elm trees.

Approaching the glade, she saw a striking woman in opulent black robes singing in the clearing. Her skin was darker than was common in Onerth, luminous, and flushed. There was an unearthly aura about her. This was no local peasant.

The part of Arianette that still clung to childlike dreams hummed to life. Was this woman, perhaps, one of those spirits she had long sought in the forgotten depths of the Greenwood? But no, that was a child's fancy and she was a woman grown now. This was just a traveler, visiting the Greenwood to witness the Rite.

Arianette stepped out from behind the trees and into the copse.

"Lady, it is not safe to venture this far into the woods alone. It is said that spirits haunt them, and there are wolves to worry about. May I be of aid to you?" Arianette asked the stranger.

The woman jerked her head up and met Arianette's questioning gaze with wide-set almond shaped eyes, dark as a predawn sky.

"Ah, Wood Witch. I hoped that we might stumble upon one another." The woman's voice was melodic as a nightingale's, carrying the rolling accent of a foreign tongue. Arianette took a few hesitant steps closer. No matter how long she gazed at the woman, she couldn't seem to get a clear glimpse of her features. But then, the dappled light of these woods had always played tricks on the eyes.

"My mother, Amabella, was the Wood Witch of this land. But she is gone and I fear I am a poor replacement. Do you have some injury that needs tending?"

"Inseoidh an aimsir," the dark woman said with an unreadable expression.

"I'm sorry? I don't understand—" Arianette began, though the language sounded familiar. The woman cut her off with a fluttering motion of her hand.

"It makes no matter, child. The night will bring answers," she said, with an odd little smile. "I shall see you at the night fires."

The woman turned away from Arianette and walked deeper into the Greenwood.

"Wait," Arianette called after her. "Who are you?"

The cloaked woman paused, turning to look back.

"My name is Lorna, Lorna Blackburn," she said. Arianette was sure she caught a mischievous glint in the

2

woman's eyes before she turned and strode off. Her form was lost amid the elongating shadows and towering trees, not even a footfall in her wake.

5

The woman in the wood tugged at Arianette's mind even as she made her way back to her cabin. She took the long way home, following the deer trail that skirted around the town proper, rather than the major thoroughfare. The town would be bustling with folk preparing for the Rite and she would rather avoid the masses. She had never had her mother's effortless way with the villagers. They mistrusted her magic, modest though it was, and Arianette sensed it whenever they chanced to meet.

She reached the split where the path and the road merged into one. A few villagers were already making their way towards the western fringes of the forest, preparing for the evening's festivities. Arianette smiled, half-hearted, at the folk as she passed. They met her smiles with indifferent nods.

All but one.

A bent and bowed old woman with skin like crumpled paper froze in her tracks as Arianette passed by. She stared at her, disgust contorting her features.

"You smell of the other side. You smell Fae touched, girl. Beware the Veil tonight," the woman hissed at her.

Arianette blinked, a chill running down her spine. The woman passed by, hissing as she hobbled down the road. She made the sign of the Goddess Xennia surreptitiously in the air as she went. Only when her form was small and distant did Arianette recover enough to continue on her way.

3

A wave of relief washed over her when the familiar sight of her cottage came into view, but she could not shake the dread that had settled over her.

The old woman had said she smelled Fae-touched and this was the night of the Rite, when the Veil between the realms was at its thinnest. Could it be that the strange women in the Greenwood *had* been from beyond the Veil ? Arianette replayed the events of the afternoon in her mind . The woman 's name . Lorna Blackburn ... Blackburn ... Blackburn ... It repeated like a chorus in her head, until at last it dawned upon her.

Arianette leapt to her feet and ran over to her pallet, digging around beneath it until she found what she sought; an illuminated book. Swirling ink on the cover proclaimed it to be *Tales of the Fae.* Such books were rarer than rare. Arianette still did not know how her mother had procured it, but since the day Amabella had given it to her on her twelfth name day it had been a prized possession. Arianette had always been preoccupied with the Fae and the world beyond the Veil. What others found terrifying, she had always found enchanting.

She flipped through the pages, pausing at the chapter headings for each Court. Earth, then Sky, Fire, then Sea. Next came Arianette's favorite, the Court of Dreams. Now, though, she skimmed straight past it. She was seeking shadow, not light. What was in a name? Certain names had power, and the one Lorna had uttered stuck in her mind as familiar.

Because, she realized, she had read it half a hundred times.

Arianette traced her fingers along the illustration. COURT OF SHADOWS- RULER - HOUSE BLACKBURN, the inscription beneath the image read.

She sat, fingering the book, lost in thought. Outside, darkness was gathering in the Greenwood. She watched the orange light flickering as the night fires were lit. Smoke wafted through her window. She should remain here, she knew, safe within the walls of her cottage. The Veil was thin and it seemed a Faery from the Shadow Court might very well lurk in the forest. But it was as if something in the woods beckoned her, called her forth to learn what secrets the night held.

Giving in to curiosity, Arianette rose and flung her cloak over her shoulders. She paused a moment at the threshold, as Amabella's words rang in her mind like her mother's ghost shared the room with her.

"The night fires are not for us. We are Wood Witches. We have a special connection to the natural powers and that makes this night a danger to us. We serve as a beacon when we venture too close to the fires. Those on the other side of the Veil might see the spark of our magic and seek to claim it for themselves. We dare not risk drawing attention to ourselves."

But her mother was dead and gone, and whatever lay in wait in the forest, the call was too strong for Arianette to resist. She stepped outside, following the narrow trail from her cottage towards the forest. Smoke rose, darker and more acrid now, as the fires raged higher and burned hotter. Despite the warmth of the midsummer air a shiver crept down Arianette's spine. She folded her arms across her chest as she walked, pulling her cloak around herself. Tonight, everything about the forest felt strange to her.

The eerie energy only grew more intense as she moved deeper into the woods. She was not sure where she was going. It was as if a powerful sixth sense was leading her. The deeper she went, the quieter it grew as she left behind the rising crescendo of the villagers' fervent prayers to Xennia. The quiet seemed only to magnify the intense pulse of energy in the atmosphere . Everything seemed taut, even Arianette's nerves.

She smelled cedar and herbs burning; verbena, willow weep, Sadie's tears, and something else. These were not the traditional herbs burned during the Rite. The air was laced with an overwhelming ephemeral aroma.

Magic, Arianette realized and froze, heart pounding.

She pressed her body against the trunk of a tree with bark so rough and gnarled that it bit through the thin cotton of her rough spun frock. Of course there was magic here, she reassured herself. It was the night of the Rite. Wasn't the purpose to celebrate and reinforce the magic that sealed the veil?

But this was not the magic of the Xennian Priestesses. This magic was raw, visceral, not the earth magic Arianette was familiar with.

She crept onward until she reached a small clearing. The dark cloaked form of Lorna Blackburn stood at its center . She was motionless , but for her lips . Strings of words in a strange tongue poured from her mouth . Arianette moved towards Lorna 's black silhouette , outlined against the back- drop of fire.

As she drew up beside her, Lorna shifted towards Aria - nette , her black robes falling away from a slender arm ringed in elaborate swirling tattoos. They appeared to be glyphs, but Arianette had no time to study them.

Lorna seized her by the hand. Her long nails bit into Arianette's calloused palm. She winced, but did not pull away as Lorna's chanting grew louder.

The language seemed to grow even more familiar as the chant went on. It wasn't as if she'd heard it before... not exactly. It was more like the words and melody were ingrained in the very fiber of her being.

Then Arianette felt her own voice welling up inside her throat and forcing its way out. The strange words tumbled from her mouth, but the chant did not sound like two voices blended in harmony. It sounded legion, like a hundred voices weaving an elaborate melody.

A Fae melody.

"*The veil between the worlds slips on the night of the Rite,*" her mother's voice whispered again in the back of her mind. "*Do not draw attention to yourself.*"

Too late.

The smoke grew ghastly thick and Arianette's eyes watered, her vision blurring. Her tongue was numb, but still she continued reciting the words. The world seemed to recede and slip away. There was only the fire and the words.

Then Lorna released Arianette's hand and grew silent. All was quiet but for the roar of the flames. Arianette turned to Lorna, eyes wide. A dozen questions died on her lips when she saw Lorna's grim expression and gritted teeth, wavering in and out of focus.

It was not a human face at all.

Before Arianette stood the glimmering visage of a Shadow Fae, struggling to hold onto her human glamour.

"You know the words, Wood Witch. Stolen child of the Fae. The Legion Queen, promised in the prophecy,"

Lorna murmured, speaking again in her accented common tongue.

Arianette backed away, a panic rising inside that threatened to choke her. Lorna's face was an impassive mask, but her movements were lightning quick. She did not step so much as shift, melding with the shadows and reappearing at Arianette's side once more.

"I am very sorry for this, Arianette Gracelilly," she whispered. "But it is time to return to the Ethereal Realms."

Then she shoved Arianette, hard, with her inhuman Faery strength, sending her hurtling headlong into the blue tinged night fire.

CHAPTER 2

THE QUEEN OF NOTHING

Though her name was written all over the annals of history, Muírgan was no one now. She was a whisper of a memory; spilled ink on the pages of time. Still, her words had the power to shift the worlds – Mortal and Fae – and her creatures slithered through the swamps, took to wing in the skies, and skulked through the forests.

It was her words and her wings that had led the shadow sorceress to the girl. It was a shame Amabella had sacrificed herself in vain trying to hide the girl. Muírgan could have used the Wood Witch. But no matter. What was done, was done, and Muírgan dared not meddle with blood magic to bring Amabella back. She could have done it. She had the power to restore life. But such spells were messy and had notoriously mixed results.

"Aciperre," Muírgan whispered. The winged form of a falcon stirred the air, landing beside Muírgan. A shadow detached itself from the bird and in its place stood a long limbed Elven man with feathery hair the hue of dried leaves and large owl round eyes.

"She has crossed the Veil, my lady, and is in the Sky Court. Though I will say, your words caused some confusion." A little smile toyed at the corners of Aciperre's lips. Muírgan sighed and gazed heavenwards.

"Oh they always do, especially with the Fae. They're so literal. And they're terrible translators." Muírgan flicked her wrist. A cluster of vines sprouted from the ceiling above her, draping down over her throne. She toyed with them as they coiled around her arm.

"Yes, well, the shadow conjuror lured her to the night fires and shoved her in. Apparently she misunderstood that part about burning." Aciperre could barely contain his grin. Muírgan's eyebrows shot up and her laughter twinkled out like bells.

"They never make things easy for themselves, do they?" Aciperre crowed.

"That they do not," Muírgan agreed. "You have done well in this, Aciperre. There will be a place of honor for you by my side when we burn the Courts and forge our unified realm." Muírgan's verdant eyes glittered. The fresh vines ensconcing her throne unfurled, twining themselves upwards around Muírgan's torso. She touched one and a tiny bud sprang open into a large white lily. Muírgan sniffed it, smiling serenely.

"And when will that be, my Queen of the realms?" Aciperre asked, eager.

"Hush, don't call me that. Not even here. One never knows where eyes and ears might be. I am the Queen of Nothing," Muírgan hissed. She liked the ring of that. It would not do for the Fae to learn that their 'prophesied one' was an Elven queen seeking to restore the Old Ways. No, that would not do.

Muírgan was content to be the Queen of Northing.

For now.

"The Dreamer sleeps still. The Legion Queen's powers are bound and she has no memories of her life on this side of the Veil. I was with Amabella when the girl was born. I have seen the chart of her stars. She is fated for star-crossed love. We must watch and wait. An opportunity to claim her will present itself in time."

Aciperre was, unsurprisingly, unhappy with this response. After centuries of life, he was still impatient, rash. It surprised Muírgan that he had not kidnapped the girl from the Sky Fae when they'd crossed over. That was his nature. She could not change his nature, but she could keep him on a short leash.

"Keep eyes on the girl, the silver lord, the golden warrior, the sorceress. But do so discreetly. Do not jeopardize my plans," Muírgan told Aciperre. He refrained from smirking, though she could tell it was difficult for him. Instead he made a stiff bow.

"As you wish, my queen," he said.

Then he whistled the high keening cry of a raptor and slipped once more into the form of his familiar, taking wing for the Court of Sky.

CHAPTER 3

BEYOND THE VEIL

Arianette lay on her back. Overhead, stars winked and twin moons grinned down at her, crescents slender as curved blades in an indigo sky.

She bolted upright and looked around. She was in an open air Courtyard. White stone spires soared overhead, gleaming like moonstone against a backdrop of smoky snowcapped mountains. She considered the possibility that she was dead. She had, after all, been shoved into a fire. Perhaps this was the afterlife. Her skull pounded, though, and her skinned knees burned. She could only hope to be relieved of such worldly pains upon she passage into the Void.

"Child, are you all right?" The voice sounded concerned. And familiar. Arianette swiveled her head to see Lorna Blackburn lowering herself to a graceful kneeling position beside her. The Faery, having shed her glamor, stopped Arianette's breath. Lorna, in her true form, was just a slip of a thing with ebony skin and indigo eyes. She looked almost identical to the Shadow Fae illustration in Arianette's book, *Tales of the Fae*, with her bat like wings folded like black leather at her shoulder blades.

"Where am I?" Arianette asked, scuttling backwards away from Lorna. She winced as the flagstones bit into the abrasions on her palms.

"Beyond the Veil," Lorna said, her voice calm. "In the Ethereal Realms."

Arianette blinked at her.

"The Court of Shadows?" she asked, voice trembling.

Lorna laughed, the sound as high and sweet as her voice had been when lifted in song.

"Of course not. Does this place look like the Court of Shadows to you?" she asked, gesturing towards the palace sprawling before them.

Arianette had to admit that it did not. There was nothing shadowy about the grand ivory arches, and embellished pillars or the life-like statues standing sentinel around the Courtyard.

"We're in the Sky Court. You may recall-"

"You don't look like a Sky Fae." Arianette countered, interrupting her.

Lorna frowned, a crease forming between her brows.

"No, I suppose I don't. But that's a tale for another day." Her tone did not leave room for argument. She moved out of her crouch and reached for Arianette's hand, pulling her to her feet in a single fluid movement.

"I'm not going anywhere with you. What were you doing in the forest? Tell me why you brought me here," Arianette declared.

"We'll have plenty of time to discuss that after you've met the Skylord," Lorna said, sounding piqued.

What on earth could the Skylord want with her, the Mortal daughter of a Wood Witch, Arianette wondered.

13

She would have asked just that, but before she got another word out, a shadow fell over them from above. The sound of beating wings became audible and Arianette glanced up to see the most majestic creature she had ever seen in her life.

Like a magnificent bird of prey, the Faery swooped down from the sky. Looking more like a statue than a man, he could have been carved from bronze. Powerfully built with the graceful sweeping antlers of a stag arcing from the crown of his head. His eyes surveyed Arianette with open curiosity; a warm amber hue with irises ringed in gold. Most striking of all, though, were his massive tawny wings shot through with gleaming crimson and ivory feathers.

"And who is this?" the antlered Fae asked in a voice that commanded attention.

"I should think that would be rather obvious Braedin," Lorna said.

"Right. Of course. This must be the prophesied Legion Queen you crossed the Veil to collect. It's just that, she looks awfully- well, she looks awfully Mortal," Braedin observed, puzzled.

"I'm not a queen," Arianette groaned. Lorna rolled her eyes.

"Oh be quiet, child. Listen, Braedin no Mortal could survive crossing the Veil through fire. Although I will admit to being a bit... underwhelmed...by her myself." Lorna said, frowning.

"Perhaps you grabbed the wrong girl?" Braedin suggested.

"Don't be a fool," Lorna snapped. "She's the right girl. Look closer. There is something about her, don't you think? There is an aura of..."

Lorna dropped off, but continued to gaze at Arianette the way a small child might peer at an unusual insect ; right before ripping its wings off.

Arianette took a few steps back away from her. She briefly considered trying to bolt and make a run for it, but dismissed the idea. She was in a castle in the clouds. Trying to scale the walls surrounding the Courtyard could only end in a fall to her death.

"So, what are your plans for her?" Braedin asked. Now he too was studying Arianette with open curiosity. She wilted beneath his gaze.

"Well, I didn't bring her back because I wanted a new pet." Lorna rubbed a finger along her lower lip. "I suspect she has untapped powers. Bound, perhaps, somehow."

"I don't have any powers," Arianette insisted. "I'm just a Wood Witch's daughter. I know the properties of plants, how to heal people with them. I'm not even any good at that! I don't even cast 'spells' and I definitely do not have any powers."

"Herb magic, spell magic, it's the same thing. If you can do one, you can learn to do the other." Lorna waved her hand, dismissive. Runes glittered around her wrist. Arianette rang her hands, looking as if she would weep.

"Lorna that's enough," Braedin admonished, picking up on Arianette's distress. He turned to address her. "Listen. I know you're frightened, but I promise we mean you no harm. Lorna's methods can sometimes be a bit … questionable, I know. But she means well. Would you let us bring you into the Sky Tower?"

Braedin gestured towards an arch to their left. It was flanked on either side by winged forms carved from marble.

They looked like avenging angels standing guard. Arianette glanced at Braedin, dubious, then sighed in capitulation.

"Fine," she conceded and allowed him to lead her into the palace.

5

The Tower of Sky was even more lavish and other-worldly inside. The floors were slate gray marble. In the center of the foyer, a grand staircase wrapped around on both sides, leading up to the pillared entrance to the grand hall. Beneath the stairways, a broad corridor led into the belly of the keep. Blue and silver tapestries depicting airborne battles lined the walls, while overhead the ceiling was decorated with all the constellations of the night sky.

Arianette sucked her breath in at the sight, spinning around to take in her surroundings.

"Welcome," Braedin said, "to the Sky Tower." A small smile played at his lips.

"I've never seen anything like it," Arianette breathed.

She couldn't linger in her thrall for long, though. Lorna was already grabbing her hand and pulling her towards the arched passageway that led into the heart of the palace.

"Come child, let's get you cleaned up, shall we?"

"I hope to see you again soon, Lady Arianette," Braedin said with a courtly bow as Lorna guided her away.

She led Arianette down a series of winding corridors. At last, they approached a small nondescript door. Lorna entered first. Arianette peeked her head in, still alert for danger.

Arianette's entire cottage could have fit inside the chamber with room to spare. To her left, glass paned double doors opened out onto a veranda. Opposite the veranda yawned a massive canopied bed , resplendent in lavender silk sheets and coverlets with a half dozen downy pillows flung about it.

"I could fetch you some tea if you'd like. Perhaps we could chat? I feel like I owe you an explanation of sorts," Lorna said, sounding hopeful.

Arianette was less than enthused about sharing tea with her captor. She turned to face Lorna.

"May I just rest for a little while?" she asked, sounding weary.

"But of course," Lorna said, though she looked crestfallen. "I'll leave you to your rest."

And so she left Arianette with an elegant curtsy, flitting from the room. Her robes swirled around her as she closed the door with a soft click.

Alone , Arianette took a deep ragged breath and tried to compose her thoughts . She wasn 't sure whether or not she was relieved. The adrenaline that had been propelling her ebbed away and she felt as if she might collapse.

But she was not ready to sleep. Not just yet.

She set about inspecting the chamber, walking first to the double doors that led out to the veranda and pulling the curtains aside. Outside, there was only a steep drop to a flagstone Courtyard lined with weapon racks and combat dummies, pale blue skies, and the jagged peaks of a mountain range sprawling as far as the eye could see. No chance of escape, not by that route, anyway.

On the far wall there was an ornate white oak writing desk. Arianette made her way over to it. She fingered the sheaf of creamy white paper, the elegant feathered quills, and vials of silver and black ink. Such fine things here in this palace, but none that did her any good. Arianette had no one to write letters to on this side of the Veil. No one even in Onerth, truth be told.

She set about opening each desk drawer until she found something useful; a bejeweled letter opener. She picked it up and hefted it in her left hand, examining the tapered end. As a weapon, it wouldn't be of much use, but for what she had in mind, it was perfect.

She walked over to the door Lorna had exited through and got down on her hands and knees. Working as quickly and quietly as she could, Arianette set about using the point of the letter opener to scratch tiny markings into the wooden door frame. She felt a bit foolish, carving Mortal runes in a land so full of true magic, powerful magic. Would her runes even work here?

When she finished warding the door against entry, Arianette moved to the double doors of the veranda, then to each of the windows, etching them into each frame. Then she looked around the room again.

Besides the bed and the writing desk, the only other piece of furniture in the room was an enormous wardrobe. So large that she wondered if she ought to place a ward on that too, for it seemed it could be the doorway to another land. Such things were regular occurrences in *Tales of the Fae.* She opened the wardrobe, afraid of what might lie within, also feeling guilty about rifling through a stranger's belongings.

To Arianette's relief, there was only clothing inside. And oh, what clothing. A confection of satin, velvet, and lace gowns in every color of the rainbow arranged on hangers. More casual leggings, tunics, and nightgowns sat folded on a set of shelves within. Arianette selected one of the simpler nightgowns and removed it from the shelf. Woven of a sky blue gauzy fabric , it was unlike anything she'd ever touched before.

She was still clad in the soiled shift she'd worn to the night fire. The strange magic of that night felt as if it had been years ago, though it couldn't have been more than a few hours since she'd crossed the Veil . Time moved differently in the Ethereal Realms . She'd heard that said before, but hadn't understood what it meant until now.

She fingered the nightgown in her hands again and glanced furtively around. Still feeling a bit guilty, she removed her own torn dress and pulled the gauzy nightgown over her head. Yawning, she made her way over to the imposing canopy bed.

Arianette was not petite. She was half a head taller than most of the other girls in the Greenwood. This bed was so large that she had to stand on tiptoes to climb into it. She wondered how a tiny Fae like Lorna would ever manage. Then she remembered. She was likely the only being here who did not have wings or magical teleportation abilities. She suddenly felt small and lost.

She did not think she would fall asleep in this strange chilly marble room, knowing Fae surrounded her, and unsure of their intentions. Pulling the sheets up to her chin and taking several deep breaths, she wondered briefly if the featherbed might be enchanted. It was so cloudlike that she feared it might be a Faery attempt to lull her into sleep and submission.

If it was, it worked. Within moments Arianette drifted off into a restless slumber.

CHAPTER 4

THE SKYLORD

Braedin left Lorna and the girl and headed straight for the Skylord's chambers. As the commander of the Sky Guard, it was his duty to report any intrigues occurring in the Court to his half-brother. This business with the Mortal certainly counted as intrigue.

The girl that intrigued Braedin. She was not at all what he had expected. She wasn't regal. Nor did she appear to be a warrior in that frail Mortal body. But there was something enchanting about her. The very air around the girl hummed with a strange intensity that *felt* like magic.

As he strode past the guards outside the Skylord's private chamber they raised their hands in a salute. Braedin returned the gesture, still lost in thought.

"Is he alone?" Braedin asked a young guard as he approached the door to Varik's solar. The guard shook his head, blushing bright scarlet.

That was enough to make the nature of his brother's company clear. Braedin had two options. He could wait for Varik to finish up with his lady friends, or he could interrupt them and say his piece. Ordinarily, Braedin was a patient man and preferred not to stir his brother's quick temper by interrupting him. News of a Mortal girl, who might be the Legion Queen, was pressing, though.

Braedin brushed past the guard's feeble protests and opened the door to the solar. He strained his eyes, peering into the dim room. Plush velvet curtains were drawn across the massive windows that encircled the Skylord's tower, blocking out both the light of the dawn and the panoramic view of the mountains.

A drunken female giggle broke the silence.

"Captain Redwing!" a high pitched female voice slurred.

Braedin scowled into the darkness. Crossing the room, he yanked the curtains open, flooding the room with watery morning light. Then he turned to his brother who was reclining on a divan. Varik's eyes were bloodshot, his hair mussed, and there were three pixies draped over him.

Varik hissed at the light streaming through the windows and squinted at Braedin, his lip curling into a scowl of irritation.

"Brother, how unexpected. I don't recall sending you an invitation to this little soiree, but as you can see there is plenty to go around." Varik gestured, encompassing the three pixies as well as the table. It was laden with cheese, caviar, dried meats, and honey buns. Half empty glasses and decanters were strewn about, as were neatly arranged rows of fairy dust.

"I'm here on business," Braedin replied stiffly. Varik snorted, reaching up to caress the bare breast of one of the pixie women who giggled again.

"You're so droll, captain," Varik complained, brushing a tangle of silverhair from his face.

"Lorna has returned with the girl," Braedin said, curt.

"What girl?" Varik asked picking up a silver goblet from the table and taking a long drink.

"The Wood Witch's daughter," Braedin explained.

Varik's eyebrow drew up into an arch.

"And?"

"Perhaps you should dismiss your company before we discuss this further." Braedin indicated the pixies with a jerk of his chin.

For a moment Varik only gazed into his wine while Braedin's frown of irritation deepened.

Varik clapped his hands together sharply.

"Ladies, I fear our time is at an end," Varik said, voice smooth as silk. The pixies whined in unison. "Get gone. Now," he ordered.

His voice had a note of command in it, and the bitter tang of magic swirled through the room as he brushed their cloying hands off him. As if enchanted, the girls rose and breezed past Braedin , then out of the chamber . Braedin closed the door behind them.

"Have a seat, brother, have a drink. Maybe a bit of dust? You look tense, as usual." Varik's tunic was wine stained and he wore no pants. Still even in his current condition, Varik maintained a silvery ethereal beauty, and an aura of intense magic. The power of his pure royal blood. A power Braedin himself would never wield. Not like Varik, anyway. He was born of the wrong father.

"No thank you. One of us needs to keep our wits about us," Braedin grumbled, lowering himself onto a settee across from Varik. Varik shrugged, indifferent.

"So the girl," he prompted. Braedin hesitated. He did not want his brother to go off on one of his tantrums.

23

He would have to be careful with how he delivered this news.

"She is not quite what we expected," Braedin began. Varik downed the rest of his wine.

"When is anything ever," he grumbled. "What's wrong with her?"

The Skylord reached across the table and poured himself another goblet of wine, spilling a good deal of it across the silver cloth. The red stain spread across the pale linen. Braedin watched it grow, a vague sense of dread filling him. He chastised himself silently. He could not go around seeing omens in every spilled glass of wine. Not with Varik around, at any rate. That would mean an omen every hour. Still a coldness lingered in his veins as he cleared his throat and went on.

"She is no warrior. A hunter, perhaps, but there's nothing martial about her. Nor does she have the bearing of a queen, or even a lady. She is, it would seem, ordinary. And Mortal. There is *something* about her, though, that I can't put my finger on."

Braedin's mind drifted, against his will, to the intoxicating scent of her. Pine, or something like it, and spice, just a touch of something sweet.

Varik drummed his fingers on his thigh, eyeing his brother. Braedin shook his head to clear the memory of her aroma.

"At any rate, whatever else she is, she is frightened and confused."

"Are you sure she's the right girl?" Varik asked.

"Lorna insists she is."

"That damnable shadow sorceress and all her bloody mysteries. I should have let her rot in her sister's Court for all the help she's been to me," Varik muttered. He leapt to his feet, staggering a bit as he rose.

"I would meet this girl," he announced. It seemed he might storm Arianette's chamber straight away. Braedin stopped his brother with a firm palm to his chest and steadied Varik when he swayed.

"Brother, you are not in any condition to—" Braedin began.

Varik cut him off.

"Who are you to tell me what sort of condition I'm in," he snarled.

"I only meant – brother you're not *clothed*."

Varik glanced down, seeming to notice his state of undress for the first time.

"Ah, indeed," he said, a bit sheepish. "Well, tonight then. I shall grant the girl an audience in my throne room at sundown. Make sure Lorna is there. This was all her bloody idea and I hold her responsible for it. For better or for worse," Varik muttered.

"As you wish," Braedin said. "But are you sure you would not rather hold the audience on the morrow?" Varik was far from sober and in no condition to conduct matters of state. But that was his own doing. The girl, however, would be weary and distraught. Braedin would have given her time to recover and get her bearings before this meeting if he could.

Varik slammed his glass onto the table and whirled to face Braedin.

"Must you question my every decision, Braedin?" he growled. Braedin sighed and lowered his head, dipping into a bow.

"My apologies, brother. I'll see that Lorna and the girl are present in the throne room at dusk."

And with that, Braedin Redwing strode from the room, forcing himself not to slam the door on his way out.

CHAPTER 5

WHERE THE LOST ARE FOUND

There were lost and forgotten places in every land. Places left to rot and ruin, inhospitable destitute places. These were the places where Muírgan sought her people. The enslaved, incarcerated, and those in hiding all over the Ethereal Realms. Slowly and surely Muírgan Vivane was finding them and gathering them to her.

Throughout the Courts and even beyond the Veil in Onerth, Muírgan's people crept, seeking the Lost Folk. They were beating wings in the night sky, scuttling beneath the sand, snapping twigs on the forest floor. When the lost were found, they brought the poor wretches back to the Broken Lands where Muírgan reigned, the ghost of a Queen, un-crowned upon a throne of her own making.

She had driven Elven iron into the heart of an ash tree, grown from the seed of the Heart of the Forest. There was no palace there now, in what had once been the Court of Dreams; only the canopy of tree boughs overhead. Gone was the great glass city, the center of learning, discourse, and dis-covery. But the land remained, just waiting to be reborn. The Broken Lands still remembered magic. This land forgotten by Mortal and Fae alike could be coaxed back to life again.

This Court had once been a wonder to behold. The shining jewel of the Ethereal Realms. A land where Fae, Mortal, and Elf were free to pursue whatever life they so desired. There had been no slavery here. No war and little hunger. It had been a last bastion of peace against the tyrannical whim of the Fae Lords.

Now the Dream Fae, those light lovely wispy creatures with nothing but music and peace in their hearts were gone. All but one. The Mortals, too, had perished, though many had slipped through the Veil, returning to Onerth from whence they had come. And the Elves... well, the Elves had lost that last fateful battle here too, had brought the whole Dream Court down around their ears with their magic.

But the Elves were not gone. Not quite.

And the eyes of every Elf, and those of every solitary Fae who had wearied of the Courts' power, who had pledged their allegiance to Muírgan, were hers to command. Even now, Aciperre's eyes were in the Court of Sky where Muírgan would make use of them to watch the girl. Amabella's daughter.

Muírgan gazed into the hollow of the ash tree, peering into the emerald stone at its center. The heart of the forest. The last relic of its kind. Once, when the Elves had ruled, there had been hundreds of Vision stones throughout the Ethereal Realms. But the Fae feared and hated them and now just this one remained.

"Let me see through the falcon's eyes," Muírgan whispered, peering into the emerald's depths.

Her vision swirled then refocused, sharper, brighter than before. She could feel Aciperre's familiar's hollow boned body perched on a railing. The man in the body of a bird was peering through a window. On the other side of the glass, Amabella's daughter, the Wood Witch's daughter, slept fitfully.

All the trouble Aciperre could be was worth it, for moments like this. Muírgan focused her mind on the slumbering girl and slipped into Arianette's dream.

CHAPTER 6

A RUDE AWAKENING

In her dream Arianette found herself in a field of scarlet flowers. A single massive white tree towered in the foreground, crimson leaves trembling on its branches, drifting slowly to the ground one by one as if relinquishing all hope. Arianette shivered. A stiff wind whispered to her in a strange language. A language that seemed somehow familiar, yet alien.

It is a dead language a voice whispered, sounding as dry and brittle as dead leaves, ancient parchment. Arianette shuddered as the words clawed at her mind. She looked around, seeking the source of the voice, but saw no one, only the leaves spiraling down in the milky light.

"Hello?" Arianette called into the gray silence. No one answered. In that strange way of dreams, the scene shifted. The tree was no longer a single tree, it multiplied into a forest of trees. This was not the Greenwood, though. These trees were far older than any in Onerth. They were vibrant resplendent trees with trunks the size of three men standing shoulder to shoulder. But something was wrong.

Smoke.

The forest was alive with voracious hungry flames, with shrieks of the dying. Burning bodies tumbled from the tree-tops. Arianette tried to flee as the smoke grew thicker and the flames leapt higher, as if they had an animalistic hunger to sate. But she could not move. She froze in place as the smoke, the flames, the very air screamed around her.

"BURN THE COURTS."

5

A yelp startled Arianette into wakefulness. Her green eyes shot open. It took a moment for her to shake the haze of the dream as she blinked, groggy, at the doorway. Lorna stood in it, looking like an angry black cat, as she hissed at the invisible barrier barring her from Arianette's chamber.

It seemed her runes had been effective after all.

"What in Xennia's name—" Lorna began. She gingered her hand towards the doorway again, then yanked it back as the air popped and sizzled. Arianette tried not to laugh.

"Well, there wasn't a lock so." Arianette shrugged. She scooted out from beneath the sheets and hopped out of bed, snatching up the letter opener she'd stashed beneath her pillow. She knelt down and added a few additional markings to the runes.

"This is Mortal magic?" Lorna asked, sounding surprised.

Arianette nodded.

"My mother taught me many wards. It should be safe to cross now." She sounded pleased with herself.

Lorna stepped across the threshold. Now that the runes were disarmed there was no sizzle of magic. She bent beside Arianette and examined the rune.

Frowning, she said, "they do not look like Mortal runes."

It seemed there were more pressing matters to attend to than what manner of magic Arianette had used to spell the door. Lorna rose and crossed the room brusquely, flinging open the wardrobe.

"You're to meet the Skylord," Lorna announced, sifting through the gowns in the wardrobe. She examined several, frowning, and putting each back.

"But it's so early," Arianette complained. Then she glanced outside, startled to see an early evening sky. Had she slept through the entire day? For a moment she thought she saw the flash of two yellow eyes peering in from the veranda, but when she looked again they were gone.

"Yes, well. The Skylord has decreed that he will meet you at sunset." Lorna shrugged. "What Varik wants, Varik gets." She pursed her lips.

"Whose gowns are these?" Arianette asked, hovering over Lorna's shoulder as she continued inspecting the contents of the wardrobe. "Won't they mind me wearing them?"

Lorna furrowed her brow. She looked sad.

"The Lady Violetta would not have minded. She was a sweet girl. She would have given you the gown off her very back. But she has no need of gowns anymore," Lorna said.

"Who is Violetta? Where is the lady now?" Arianette asked. There was a mournfulness in Lorna's tone that made it seem that Violetta, whoever she was, wasn't coming back.

"Varik's sister. The crown Princess. She is gone to the Void now." Lorna met Arianette's gaze and there was a sparkle behind her eyes that might have been tears. Or perhaps just a trick of the light.

32

"Oh. I'm sorry. Tell me, how is it that Fae, ehm...die? Being immortal and all," Arianette asked, fidgeting.

Lorna waved a hand dismissively, revealing her rune encircled arm again.

"We do not die as humans do. We do not age, or sicken, or grow frail. But we can be unmade. It is difficult to send us to the Void, but not impossible. Iron. Ash. Spell craft. There is also... but we'll talk about that later, for now we need to get you ready for the Skylord." Lorna's voice was choked for a moment.

She was silent as she sifted through the garments in the closet. Then she brightened.

"This one, I think," she said, pulling it from the hanger.

The gown was far finer than anything Arianette had ever owned, or even laid eyes on in Onerth. Backless, to accommodate Lady Violetta's wings, which she herself lacked, it was a deep violet hue with a low intimidating V neck. The slim fitting bodice was inlaid with tiny amethyst gems.

Arianette frowned doubtfully at Lorna.

"Isn't there something a bit less—" she paused.

"You know, something simpler?" Arianette gestured towards the wardrobe. Lorna shook her head emphatically.

"We need to *impress* Lord Varik," she insisted, thrusting the dress at Arianette, whose frown only deepened upon closer inspection.

"I don't think this—" Arianette tried again, but Lorna cut her off.

"I didn't ask you what you thought. I told you to put it on. I've been Varik's advisor for years. I know what he likes. If you don't make a good first impression, I can assure you,

you'll never see your pastoral little Greenwood again. And that's what you want isn't it? To go home?"

Arianette stiffened at the mention of her home. It wasn't as if she'd left much behind in the Greenwood. Her mother was dead and the townsfolk had no love for her. But she had called it home for as long as she could remember, and felt a pang of loss at the idea of never seeing it again. She was also certain she did not want to disappoint this Skylord, a Fae Prince. What might the punishment be? A lifetime of gla-mored servitude , perhaps , or maybe living out the rest of her Mortal days in a dungeon?

She took the gown from Lorna and clutched it to her chest, feeling dazed. Even now the dream hung over her like a dark veil. Why did it feel so familiar? Like it wasn't a dream at all; like it had happened to her. But that was impossible. She had never run through a burning forest in the Ethereal Realms. There had been no such red leafed tree. She would remember something like that, wouldn't she?

But then there had always been something odd about Arianette 's childhood memories . The more she tried to focus on them , the more illusory they became . It had always been this way, and she had never thought much of it, but now, with all that had happened she wondered … Why didn't she remember her youth? And why did she feel like she did remember both the alien forest in her dreams and Lorna's strange tongue?

She shook her head, throwing off the unnerving thoughts. Whatever pieces were missing from her past, her future held the Skylord. Perhaps he would see that there was some mistake, that she was not this Queen they sought, and take pity on her. Perhaps he would send her home.

"We haven't got all night," Lorna said, glaring at her.

Arianette sighed.

"A little privacy?" she grumbled, snatching the dress from Lorna and nudging her chin towards the door.

Lorna muttered something about shy Mortals under her breath. But she obliged Arianette and stepped out of the room.

The gown was intimidating. Arianette could not even imagine herself wearing something so fine or so risqué. With a sigh, she slipped it over her head, shimmying into it with some difficulty. It was tight in the hips and her breasts threatened to spill out of the low cut bodice. The fabric seemed to conform to her body otherwise though, and she wondered if Lorna had enchanted it to cling where it did. The neckline plunged so low that Arianette blushed just thinking about all that she would reveal to this Skylord.

In the wardrobe she found a pair of silvery satin slippers inset with aquamarine jewels and crystal heels. She slipped her feet into them. These too were a perfect fit, though she was so used to her worn and beaten calfskin boots that she feared she might stumble in these impractical things. She afelt half naked.

A perfunctory knock came upon the door. Lorna didn't wait for Arianette to respond before barging back into the room.

"Are you ready yet?" she bemoaned.

Arianette considered strangling her. Instead, she turned around and shot her most disgruntled look at Lorna.

"Oh my, you clean up well," Lorna said, ignoring the venomous expression on Arianette's face. She took Arianette's hand and led her over to a full length looking glass on the far wall.

"I feel ridiculous," Arianette said, pursing her lips and rolling her eyes.

Then she caught sight of her reflection and stared at herself in wonder. She looked nothing like the Wood Witch's daughter from the Greenwood who'd been dragged across the Veil.

Her hair fell in gentle curling scarlet rivulets that spilled over her bare shoulders. Despite her initial uncertainty, the gown hugged Arianette's curves in all the right places. She had always felt top heavy and frumpy in her rough spun pocketed frocks, but this gown dipped in at the waist creating the illusion of a perfect hourglass shape. The neckline, though, was as alarmingly revealing as she'd feared. Her pale breasts peeked over the bodice and she had to quell the urge to clasp her arms around her chest to cover herself.

"I think you're ready," Lorna said. "But first a few things you should know." She gnawed on her violet lip.

"I brought you here because of a prophecy, as you know. But there is also a curse, a punishment for the part we played during the Great War," Lorna said.

Arianette raised her eyebrows. Was the Sky Court still being punished for standing with the Elves and the Dreamers?

"What sort of a curse?"

"Creatures called the Accursed have been encroaching upon the Court of Sky. They're aggressive."

"Creatures?" Arianette asked frowning. Lorna fluttered her hand, her bat like wings beating the air.

36

"That's a conversation for another time. Just know that this curse, these creatures, are a source of anxiety for the Skylord. There is also the matter of my sister, Ereda, who insists on amassing her armies right on our doorstep."

Arianette's mind spun back to her book, *Tales of the Fae*. Ereda Blackburn was the ruler of the Shadow Court. She furrowed her brow, trying to piece it together. That must mean Lorna was her sister. But why was Lorna in the Sky Court?

Lorna went on.

"Enemies besiege us on all sides and this has fallen most unexpectedly upon the Skylord's shoulders. Varik Skyborn is young, untried, frustrated. What I'm trying to say is that, well, he can be a bit...cranky."

Arianette could not help but laugh.

"Cranky?" she repeated back. That was the word Lorna chose to describe the Lord of the Court of Sky?

"Yes. And wanton," Lorna muttered.

Arianette gnawed on a fingernail. Lorna gently swatted her hand away from her mouth.

"Don't do that, you'll ruin your nail beds," she scolded. "Just try to act powerful," Lorna suggested.

Arianette rolled her eyes.

"But I'm not powerful. I told you that. I'm just the—"

"Daughter of a Wood Witch. So you've said. Just pretend." Lorna sighed. "Let's go then shall we? Don't want to be late!" Irritating feigned cheerfulness forced its way into Lorna's voice and Arianette gritted her teeth to avoid saying something she might regret.

She straightened the folds of her gown and yanked the neckline up as high as she could. Then she took a deep breath, lifting her chin.

"Let's get this over with," she said.

Lorna smiled, looking relieved that Arianette had chosen not to put up a fight. She swept from the room, her black leathery wings fluttering. Arianette followed close behind. The corridors of the Sky Keep were just as winding as she'd thought the day before. Mazelike, Arianette would be lost without Lorna to guide her. She could find her way out of any forest or field with the sun, moon, and trees to guide her, but within these unfamiliar walls she was at a loss.

They passed many Fae and lesser Faeries in the halls. At this hour of the evening, the palace was teeming with activity. Arianette did her best not to ogle them, but the variety fascinated her. Most striking were the guards clad in pale blue and silver fighting leathers with long swords in silvery scabbards strapped to their backs. Each had fantastic wings in all sorts of shapes and colors, no two alike. They stood immobile as statues, not even blinking as Lorna and Arianette passed.

"Sky Guards," Lorna explained, noticing how the armed Fae had caught Arianette's attention. "The Skylord's personal militia. Their sole function is to protect the Skylord at all costs, they are some of the most powerful Wind Talkers in the Court, and they're also quite skilled in arms. No one you want to tangle with, so do stop staring."

Arianette averted her eyes from the Sky Guards, only to become entranced by a host of little insectile Faeries with butterfly wings and glowing yellow skin. They scuttled down the corridors bearing trays of food, buckets, and tiny feather dusters. Lorna's violet lips quirked up into a smile.

"Pixies," she said. She did not slow her pace. "Unlike some of the more barbaric Courts, the Sky Court has never used Mortal or Elven slaves. The pixies are solitary Fae, not members of our Court, but we offer them protection within the walls of the palace for their service. There has been an influx of them as the surrounding lands have grown more dangerous."

Arianette felt a little bit relieved. If she had to be stranded in the Ethereal Realms, at least she hadn't wound up in a Court where Mortal slavery was commonplace.

Finally they arrived at a fancifully carved set of arched double doors with Sky Guards standing at attention on either side.

"Alright, now try to wipe that silly doe-eyed look off your face . It's liable to irritate Varik ," Lorna hissed , nodding to the guards who proceeded to swing open the doors.

CHAPTER 7

A HARD BARGAIN

Arianette tried not to appear dazzled as they passed through the doorway, but it was a struggle she could not win. The throne room was painted in the hue of a morning sky, with dreamy clouds of mother-of-pearl inlay streaking the walls and high cathedral ceilings. She gazed in wonder at her surroundings. Then her eyes fell upon the massive white marble throne.

The Skylord lounged upon the dais, inhumanly beautiful. Arianette's breath caught in her throat at the sight of him. He sat with one leg draped casually over the arm of the throne, gazing into the depths of a crystal goblet. His skin was paler than ivory, his features chiseled flawlessly into a face like moonstone. His long hair was ice blue streaked with the same silver that flecked his crystal eyes.

As she and Lorna moved towards him, he rose from his throne, wings extended out behind him. Their span was massive, their crystalline surface shot through with metallic whorls and dusted with shimmering downy feathers.

Lorna nudged Arianette hard in the ribs with her elbow, then yanked on her sleeve as she dropped into a low elegant curtsy. Arianette struggled to follow sort, but her attempt was clumsy in her high heeled shoes and she nearly toppled over.

Lorna snorted at the misstep, but the Skylord did not seem to notice Arianette's lack of etiquette. As he swooped down from the dais, magic so strong that it made her bones tingle wafted off of him in waves. Arianette ground her teeth against its pull.

"You seem nervous," Varik drawled. "Wine?" He thrust his chalice at her. Unsure how to politely decline, Arianette blushed and stammered. Faery wine was something no Mortal could partake in without fear of losing their mind. Lorna came to her rescue.

"No wine, Varik," she said, curtly dismissing his offer. "May I present you Arianette Gracelilly the –"

"Mortal?" he mused, his eyebrows lifting.

"Daughter of the Wood Witch of the Greenwood," Lorna finished.

Varik prowled around Arianette in a close circle, examining her as if she were a recently acquired piece of furniture. Then he brought his face close to hers, inhaling, like an animal scenting his prey. He ran a be-ringed hand over her collarbone and a shiver raced through Arianette, a shudder of fear mingled with desire.

She tensed as his fingers crept up her neck then breezed around her throat, but Varik let his hand drop, drawing around in front of her again. His silver flecked eyes locked with hers and a strange sensation shot up her spine. It was as if something inside her were clawing to break free. Her lips parted, saliva welling up in her traitorous mouth.

"Varik, stop." Lorna's voice rang out in the throne room. Both the Skylord and Arianette blinked, startled out of their reverie at the sound. He continued to look at her strangely, though, as if both bewildered and bewitched by her presence.

Varik's lips curled into an amused half smile. Golden liquid sloshed over the rim of his goblet, and Arianette realized that Varik seemed unsteady. His startling eyes were drifting in and out of focus, violet pupils dilating.

He was intoxicated, Arianette realized. Very intoxicated.

"Lorna is no fun," Varik declared. His tone was light but his expression was hard.

"She's also terrible at breaking curses or you wouldn't have to be here." Varik took another gulp of wine, glancing at Lorna, accusation in his eyes. Lorna dipped her head at Varik, an unspoken apology for her failure.

"That's neither here nor there, though is it? *You* my lady are here, for better or for worse. Do you know, you're probably the first Mortal in the Sky Court since the Culling? Most of your kind fled. Those who weren't culled that is. Assuming you are, in fact, a Mortal as my brother and Lorna claim."

There was no menace in his tone but Arianette swallowed hard all the same. Every man and woman in Onerth had heard the tales of the Culling. The rulers of the Faerie Courts, concerned that the rampant fertility of Mortals was affecting the purity of their bloodlines, decreed that all humans were banished. Elves too, though from the stories precious few of those were left by then, the Elves having been victims of cleansing by the Fae for centuries. Any Mortals or Elves who chose not to heed the warnings and leave the Ethereal Realms were systematically eradicated, or enslaved. Only the Court of Sky and the Court of Dreams had stood against the purging.

"Don't worry, Arianette, I've no intention of harming you or letting anyone else do so. You intrigue me." Varik drew one finger along her cheekbone and Arianette trembled at the touch. "Though I'm sure the Shadow Empress Ereda would enjoy feasting on your nightmares, given the chance," Varik added. Arianette swiveled her head to look at Lorna.

Lorna pursed her lips and furrowed her brow. There was clearly no love lost between her and her sister.

Varik's smile was smooth.

"I actually find it rather... special to have a Mortal in my Court." He arched a silver eyebrow. "I've heard so many things about you. The prophesied Legion Queen, who will unite the Realms once more. Right here in my very own throne room. Please, consider this your home until we determine just how you can be of use to us. It will be my pleasure to host you. Indefinitely."

His smile remained benevolent, but his words struck dread into the pit of Arianette's stomach. Her knees felt weak and her stomach heaved. Her heart was beating too fast.

"Sir, you must let me go home. I have no powers, I'm not even a genuine Wood Witch, just the daughter of one. I assure you, I am *not* this Legion Queen. I'm the farthest thing from royalty in the world. You cannot mean to make me stay—"

Varik cocked his head at Arianette, frowning.

"I do not go by sir. You may call me 'Your Majesty.' And I can do whatever I want. I'm the Skylord after all," he said with a chuckle, raising his glass in a mock salute.

His scowl shifted into a smirk that spread across his flawless face.

43

"I'll tell you what, though, *Mortal*. I propose a geis. Since you believe that there is some mistake, that you are *not* the prophesied Queen, let us make a bargain," Varik announced, his voice as slick as oil and as sweet as spun sugar. Arianette stiffened. Cutting a deal with the Fae was not something to undertake lightly.

"No tricks," Arianette warned, narrowing her eyes.

"No tricks." Varik agreed. "On my honor." He raised his right hand and placed it on his heart.

"What are the stipulations of this bargain?" Arianette's voice trembled as she spoke. She did not have much faith in this Skylord Varik's honor... but she also knew the Fae would not break a geis. This might be an out for her, if she was careful and smart about it.

"You stay here, in the Sky Court, until we can determine if you are the Queen who was promised to us." His blue eyes glittered. "If it turns out you are not, Lorna will deliver you home on the next new moon when she can part the Veil again. Simple." He paused, for dramatic effect. Arianette barely quelled the impulse to roll her eyes.

"And if I do turn out to be this Legion Queen of yours?" It was always best to know exactly what one was getting herself into when dealing with Faeries.

"If you *are* the prophesied one, you will stay and weather this storm. You will fight beside us in our battles. You will stand with the Court of Sky." Varik cleared his throat. "And you will soul-fast yourself to me and become my Lady Consort."

He added this last bit so offhanded that Arianette thought she surely must have misheard him. Even Lorna looked shocked as she blinked, slack jawed, at Varik.

"Your Lady Consort?" Arianette repeated back.

"Varik, have you gone mad?" Lorna demanded.

"Well, if she truly is nothing more than a girl with a bit of woodland magic in her Mortal veins, she has nothing to worry about." Varik shrugged his shoulders

"Why would you want me as your Lady Consort?" Arianette asked, bewildered.

Varik set his goblet down. In one quicksilver movement he was so close to Arianette that she could smell the wine on his breath and feel the hot magic streaming off of him. He inhaled, then exhaled slowly onto Arianette's neck. Her skin prickled. It was as if the very air he breathed was magic laden, as if it would crawl beneath her skin and seep into her being.

She moved to step away from Varik, but he was too inhumanly quick. He brought his arm around, looping it behind her back and pulling her close to him in what was nearly an embrace.

"I can smell the power in you," he whispered. His voice was husky as he spoke the words into the hollow of her collarbone. Then he pulled back and they locked eyes again. "And any man with eyes could see your beauty."

Arianette drew a shaky breath.

"I have no powers," she insisted, but her voice came out ragged. She sounded uncertain.

"Then you should have no qualms about agreeing to my bargain," the Skylord pressed.

Arianette stood frozen for a moment, unable to break free from Varik's gaze. She struggled to master her breathing.

Then she slowly nodded.

"I accept your terms, Lord Skyborn," she whispered.

Lorna began muttering about stupid Mortals who talk too much under her breath. Then she grabbed Arianette by the elbow, dragging her slowly backwards, extricating her from Varik's embrace.

"I'm quite sure she will enjoy your hospitality, then my Lord," Lorna said. "But perhaps she is a bit weary after all this activity," she finished through gritted teeth.

Arianette didn't protest. She didn't utter a word. She just kept gazing into Varik's silver and blue eyes wondering what she'd just gotten herself into.

"Take her to her chamber then. And have some of those little pixie girls sent up to amuse me. The pretty ones," he ordered.

"Yes, your majesty," Lorna said, dropping into another low curtsey and yanking Arianette by the elbow again. Arianette stumbled into another failed attempt at a curtsey.

With some effort, she dragged her eyes away from Varik's and glanced at Lorna who looked tense but resigned. It seemed the meeting was over. And Varik had gotten exactly what he'd wanted.

Arianette was led out of the throne room. Lorna's expression made it perfectly clear that she was less than pleased with how this situation had played out.

"Oh and Lorna," Varik's voice echoed off the stone walls, calling after them. "Find out what she is. The girl reeks of magic and it's not simple herb lore. It's potent magic, but it's not Fae magic. Not entirely anyway."

"Yes, your majesty, of course," Lorna agreed.

Arianette was mute and despondent as Lorna led her out of the throne room, back through the corridors, and up a set of stairs. If the guards lining the corridors were at all

46

curious about Arianette's presence in the Court none showed it. They all stared straight ahead, wings tucked in at the shoulders, swords brandished on their silver studded belts.

Finally, Lorna delivered her to the doorway of Violetta's massive ornate bedchamber, which was, it seemed, to be Arianette's lodging for the time being. She prattled on for a while, but Arianette was unresponsive, lost deep in her own thoughts.

Why did everyone here seem to think she possessed some powerful magic? Yes, she could brew a drought or use a power word to make a wound heal more quickly... but even as far as Wood Witches went, she was a poor one. Her mother, Amabella, had been an exceptional healer, could do things Arianette could only dream of. Arianette's magic was weak. She had always struggled with even the smallest spells. There was none of Amabella's ease in her spell work.

"Arianette, are you listening to me?" Lorna asked, sounding exasperated. Arianette blinked, coming back out of her thoughts.

"I'm sorry what?"

Lorna sighed.

"I asked if you need anything, if there's anything I can do to make you more comfortable."

"You can take me home." Tears welled up in Arianette's eyes and she fought to keep them contained. Lorna's expression was wistful. She reached out to tuck a stray tendril of fiery hair behind Arianette's ear, almost tenderly.

"Oh child, I cannot. Even if I wanted to, even if the Skylord did not forbid it. It is not like the old days. You cannot simply part the veil and travel between the worlds like you once could. There was powerful magic used after the Culling to seal the Veil. It is only possible on the new moon and high celestial days. And even then it is… difficult."

Lorna sounded apologetic and her hand lingered on Arianette's cheek. Arianette brushed the hand away, roughly, fighting back more tears.

"Come," Lorna said softly. "Let us talk."

For a moment Arianette looked as if she would resist. Then she plunked herself down on the bed and gestured for Lorna to sit beside her.

"I would tell you a story. A tale of what was, and what some say will be. At its heart is the reason you are here. Would you hear it, Arianette Gracelilly, daughter of the Wood Witch Amabella Gracelilly?" Lorna asked. Arianette was a little surprised that Lorna knew her mother's name, but she didn't let on.

"I would hear it." She tucked her feet cross legged beneath her as Lorna began her tale.

CHAPTER 8

THE COST OF LOSS

"I am sure you are familiar with my sister, Ereda Blackburn the Shadow Empress." Lorna began. "The Culling was her idea, her grand plan. She claimed the goal of the Culling was to destroy the Elves, who she contended were fearsome and dangerous and had resisted Fae rule at every turn . They were , she claimed , a threat to our very survival . She would also have done with the Mortals , whose blood had for too long been mingling with and diluting the Fae bloodlines . Looking back, though , I do not think the Elves or the Mortals were Ereda's true target. They were scape- goats, a means to an end."

Lorna's eyes were glassy, her face set in a grimace, but she went on all the same.

"It was only the Dreamers who supported the Elven Kingdom's right to exist and the Mortals' right to live free. The Courts of Shadow and Dream had been at odds since time immemorial, since the first days of the Fae conquest of the Ethereal Realms. Why? I cannot say. I'm sure you have heard how petty the Fae Lords can be, and you've met Varik, who is a wonderful example."

Arianette blanched. She did not want to imagine what being at odds with the vain self-important Skylord she'd met in the throne room might be like.

"So Ereda gathered the other Fae Lords for a Reckoning. This is how the Fae decide upon matters that affect all of the Courts." Lorna explained. Arianette opened her mouth to ask a question, but Lorna silenced her with a look.

"All that matters about the Reckoning is the result. Anuin and Alarkin, twin rulers of the Earth Court, Nimione of the Sea Court, and, albeit grudgingly, Asheron of the Court of Flames sided with Ereda in her motion to enact the Culling. The Court of Dreams, led by Somnium, stood firm against it. The Sky Court, whose ruler at the time was Lord Vargas, Varik's father allied with the Dreamers. He was wed and bonded to Lady Solara, Somnium's sister. Some believe Solara cast an enchantment on Vargas. Others think Vargas was soft-hearted. Whatever the case, the Skylord sided with the Dreamers in defying the Edict of Culling. And so began the War of the Courts." Lorna paused.

"Everyone knows the story of the Great War," Arianette said, impatient. "What has that to do with me?" She well knew the story. It didn't seem the least bit relevant to Arianette's current plight as a captive in the Ethereal Realms.

Lorna sighed.

"As you know, in the conflict's aftermath, they destroyed the Court of Dreams. Not the Court of Shadows as so many would have you believe. The Elves and the Dreamers themselves destroyed it when they sealed the Veil. Ereda was furious at having her final vengeance snatched from her hands. She took this anger out on the Sky Fae, allies of the Dreamers. She used the stolen knowledge of Elven magic that she'd gleaned from her Elven slaves to cast the hex that created the Accursed."

"Lorna, I'll be honest. I don't care about your wars or your hexes or the ill feelings between the Fae Courts. All I want is to go home. To go back across the Veil and live in my little cabin in the Greenwood. I want to mix my potions and heal the villagers."

Lorna snapped her head up and glared at Arianette.

"Has it occurred to you might be here for a reason? That there might be something bigger than you going on here that you must play a role in? By rights, you should have died in that fire. That you didn't means you're meant to take part in this. Maybe you should try thinking about someone other than yourself."

Arianette's anger flared. She jumped off the bed and flung her arms in the air.

"Who are you to tell me what to do and how to feel? You've never been torn away from your entire life, your entire world, everything you've ever known," Arianette fumed.

Lorna stared at her, the irritation gone. Now she just looked sad.

"Oh but I have," she said, but didn't seem willing to elaborate. Instead she thrust a yellowing scroll at Arianette.

"What's this?" Arianette asked.

"An ancient Elven prophecy," Lorna said as if this were the most natural thing in the world, as if everyone carried ancient prophecies around in the pockets of their robes.

Arianette squinted at the vellum. The twists and swirls of the script were beautiful, but no alphabet that she could make sense of. There was, once again, something familiar about the strange elaborate scrawl though. As if a memory that would explain why she seemed to recognize it were right there, but buried so deeply that she could not touch upon it.

The sensation was disconcerting.

"It's in Elven," Lorna explained. "The forgotten language of a dead people." She tossed her jet and gold hair and surprised Arianette with a broad smile.

"Fortunately, we love dead things in the Shadow Court. And I have always been partial to dead languages."

Arianette blinked at her.

"So you truly are Shadow Fae?" she asked, the prophecy forgotten.

Lorna muttered an unfamiliar word and suddenly dissolved into a thick black smoke. When the smoke dissipated Lorna stood on the opposite end of the room.

"I told you I was Ereda Blackburn's sister," she said, stretching her membranous black wings to their full span. The room darkened. Shadows seemed to slither away from the walls, pooling at Lorna's feet, crawling up to cloak her in a diaphanous veil of darkness.

"I only thought-" Lorna cut Arianette off with a sharp wave of her bejeweled fingers.

"I know what you thought. The same thing all Mortals think. The shadow Court is all dark scary things that go bump in the night. Here is some advice. Don't judge a Faery based on their Court. Look at Varik and Braedin. They're like night and day and they're both Sky Fae. Just because the Empress of the Court of Shadows is an insufferable demon, doesn't mean that we all are. Many of us fled and sought sanctuary in the other Courts when Ereda came into her power.

My point with this little demonstration is we must all choose a side. Will you run back to your little woodland hide away without even trying to do what is right? Will you wait there for my sister to set her sights on destroying Onerth too? Because, make no mistake, unchecked she will try to shatter the Veil." Lorna's eyes burned into Arianette. "Or will you listen to the Prophecy, witness what we face, and then make your decision?"

Arianette frowned. For a moment she considered denying her, insisting that she wanted nothing to do with these Fae and their plight. In the end, Arianette sighed and relented.

"I will listen," she conceded.

"Excellent." Lorna pointed at the scroll Arianette held.

"The problem is there is almost nobody around who reads fluent Elven anymore. The few Elves who survived the Culling are all enslaved. Most were born in chains and never even learned their own language. Those who do recall it have sworn never to speak it again, at penalty of death. That's how powerful Elven spells are, how fearful of them the Fae are," Lorna explained.

"So, there are parts of this prophecy I understand, and parts that mean next to nothing to me. And then there are the parts I was sure I had figured out, but it seems I was wrong about." Lorna cast an appraising glance at Arianette. "Like you, for example."

Arianette rolled her eyes.

"All right, I'll bite. What did you think it said about me?"

The scroll felt strange in Arianette's hands; warm and almost as if it were reverberating. Lorna's words about the strength of Elven magic made Arianette wonder if an inanimate object could be infused with power. What dark words were inscribed in this fanciful red ink? She suddenly had the peculiar sensation that the scroll was whispering to her fingertips. She thrust the thing back at Lorna, who accepted it, opening it up and laying it flat on the bed.

"This part here." Lorna drew a black nailed fingertip along some lines of text in the middle of the document. "The prophecy says that the Legion Queen, the daughter lost and forgotten in the Mortal realm, will come to end the Accursed and reunite the Ethereal Realms in their darkest hour. And long would she reign over all the lands. Or something to that effect."

"All this talk of the Legion Queen. What does that even mean? And has it occurred to you I am no Queen? Only the simple daughter of..." Arianette dropped off, making the connection.

She laughed. It was a forced manic laughter that might turn to tears at any moment. Varik's words in the throne room, the strange bargain he had struck, suddenly made perfect sense. He was hedging his bets she was some great warrior Queen. And he wanted to rule her kingdom.

Lorna smile was wan.

"So, you see now. But there is more. I know it sounds a bit crazy. Just humor me for a moment. I believe you are the Legion Queen, but I believe there is some binding on you constricting your powers so that even you yourself are not aware of what you are. Can you recall anything strange from your childhood? Any ritual your mother might have performed when you were young?"

Arianette bit her lip.

"No. Nothing. I had a perfectly normal childhood in the Greenwood," Arianette lied.

She would not tell Lorna about the gaps in her memory, about the fact that what she recalled from her youth seemed somehow false. As if the memories were not her own, but had been planted there by someone else.

Lorna sighed.

"Will you at least see this through with me, at least for a little while? Let me show you the Accursed so you can see what we face. You are stuck here at least until the new moon, anyway."

"Fine," Arianette grumbled. It wasn't like she had anything better to do, trapped here as she was. And she had to admit, she was at least a little bit curious about these Accursed Lorna spoke of.

"Thank you, Arianette." Lorna said, inclining her head to Arianette. "Sleep well. You have been through much, and there is more, I think, yet to come. You will need your rest."

CHAPTER 9

THE ACCURSED

Arianette slept that night, a sweet dreamless sleep. She awoke to the sound of swordplay filtering in from the veranda. For a moment, she panicked, her mind unable to grasp her surroundings. Then she heard the sound of laughter that she recognized to be Braedin's.

Everything came rushing back.

She tiptoed over to the balcony, opened the double doors, and stepped out into the warm bright sun of mid-morning. Peering over the railing she saw two men sparring in the courtyard below. Braedin Redwing and Varik Skyborn faced off with their gleaming silver swords. Both were shirtless and winded, though Varik looked the worse for the exertion. His lithe form moved across the marble court-yard with all the feline grace of a panther . His movements were lightning quick, but his blue lips were set in a thin grim line of determination as he jabbed and parried Braedin's strokes.

Braedin, with his bronze skin and golden hair, didn't even seem winded by the onslaught of blows. He was larger than Varik with broader shoulders and a longer reach. While not as quick, he fought with a steady and relentless tenacity.

He blocked Varik's quick flurry of strikes, then pushed him back with powerful, measured strokes of his own.

Arianette couldn't take her eyes off of them. She watched the fighting, riveted by the way they moved in that strange lethal dance, until Braedin rounded on Varik, thrusting his sword arm upward to knock Varik's blade aside. Then Braedin planted his longsword mere inches from his brother's neck.

Varik snarled and swatted Braedin's sword, bending to retrieve his own blade and sheathing it.

"You're out of practice, brother," Braedin said amiably. Varik bent over, hands resting on his thighs, panting.

"Yes, well, I've had more practice wielding my other sword of late." Varik made a crude gesture towards his groin and color crept into Arianette's cheeks.

Braedin laughed, moving to pat Varik on the back. With a sweeping motion like quicksilver, Varik whipped his dagger from his belt. In a flash he had brought it to Braedin's throat, then froze, the blade hovering above his jugular.

"Perhaps you're the one out of practice, Braedin. Remember, never let your guard down," Varik teased with a quick wink. Then he flicked his wrist, sending his dagger flipping through the air and landing in its sheath. A small "ah" escaped Arianette's lips at the blinding speed of the blade.

Both men turned startled faces up to see her standing on the balcony, clad only in a nightgown, red hair streaming in the gentle breeze, a look of wonder on her face.

"It seems we have a voyeur in the tower," Varik announced, a grin toying at his lips.

"Aye. And now she's seen which of us can wield a sword... and which is more accustomed to daggers," Braedin said with a hearty laugh.

Arianette balked, her face burning with humiliation at being caught watching the two of them. She quickly turned on her heel, scampering back into her chambers, leaving both men staring up at the place where she had been.

She spent the better part of an hour hiding in her chambers hoping she might simply die of embarrassment. She changed into a pair of silvery leather leggings and a simple lavender tunic she found in the wardrobe.

A tray full of food; juicy nectarines, figs, and fresh baked bread, had appeared on the writing desk while she'd been on the balcony as if by magic. It seemed everything was magical here, except for Arianette. At first she picked at the food, worried that it might be enchanted. Once she'd eaten a fig and suffered no ill effects, though, she dug into it, voracious. She had not eaten since she'd crossed the Veil and found herself quite famished now that her adrenaline had worn off.

She was still stuffing her face when there came a sharp knock on her door. Already Arianette recognized the sound.

"Come in," she called through a mouthful of bread.

Lorna opened the door and peered in.

"It's not warded this time," Arianette assured her. She'd been far too tired to even think about warding the door before she'd fallen asleep the night before.

"Are you ready?" Lorna asked as she stepped, hesitantly to Arianette's delight, into the room.

"Ready for what?" Arianette asked, popping another fig into her mouth.

"To see the Accursed."

Arianette groaned. She'd almost forgotten that she'd agreed to that.

"I suppose," she grumbled.

"Come then."

They made their way through the palace's labyrinthine corridors once more, eventually stepping out into a courtyard similar to the one Arianette had found herself in upon her arrival in the Ethereal Realms. She would've assumed it was the same Courtyard , if the statuary hadn't been different.

"So, where exactly are we going?" Arianette asked.

"To the pit," Lorna said.

Arianette didn't like the sound of that.

"Where's the pit?"

"At the bottom of the mountain."

Arianette blanched.

"And how are we going to get down there?" She hoped Lorna didn't have any ideas about turning her into shadowy ether and teleporting her.

Just then, Arianette heard a familiar flapping of wings she recognized to be Braedin's. He swooped down from the clouds and landed beside them, tossing Arianette a grin.

"He will carry you," Lorna informed her. Arianette shot her a desperate look. It was bad enough that Braedin had caught her spying on him, now he was going to carry her around like she was a child?

"Isn't there a path or something?" she groaned.

Braedin chuckled.

"There is, but I don't think you want to take that route." He pointed to a crevice in the mountain wall where a narrow rock cut wound its way down to the valley below. It exhausted Arianette just looking at it.

"Perhaps not," she conceded grudgingly.

"Don't worry. I'll hold onto you tight." Arianette squealed as Braedin lifted her into his arms. "Close your eyes if you're afraid," he whispered into her hair, inhaling the fresh spicy aroma of her again.

He stretched his tawny gold dusted wings wide. At first Arianette kept her face buried in Braedin's chest, eyes jammed closed, arms rigid and clinging. But slowly she relaxed into the rhythmic motion his wings beat out against the sky. Her muscles gradually became less tense and she lifted her head. Braedon smiled at her.

The spires of gleaming white soared far above them. From the air, Arianette could see that the Sky Palace was carved into the very peaks of the mountains themselves. Its gleaming white pinnacles spiraled up against the backdrop of the blue sky as they descended. Overhead a single golden falcon soared in graceful figure eights.

"Don't worry. This isn't my first landing," Braedin said winking at her as they descended towards a massive crevasse, rather like the moats at Onerthian fortresses, which ringed the base of the castle. His landing was so gentle that Arianette barely noticed it when he touched down. He set her on her feet.

"That wasn't so bad, was it?" Braedin teased as Lorna materialized beside them.

"Better than doing that." Arianette still found that shadowy teleportation thing of Lorna's unnerving. Braedin laughed.

"I agree."

60

"What's so funny?" Lorna asked as Arianette tried to suppress a giggle. Braedin waved her off, then turned serious.

"Shall we?" He gestured towards the stony rim overlooking the chasm. Lorna nodded, looking grim. They headed towards the ledge, Arianette lagging. Drawing up to the edge, they stood at the top of an embankment and gazed down into the pit. Braedin and Lorna both frowned. Arianette peeked over.

The sight below made her shudder. Her mouth formed a wide O of horror as she gazed down at the mass of writhing bodies in the pit. Their skin was dull gray with a greenish tint. Their flesh looked as if it were decaying and their clothing was all bloodstained and in tatters. Even as far away they were, the Accursed seemed to sense their little party. Turning their faces skyward as if they were a single unit, the mass of wretched bodies gazed up at the bluff with eerie scarlet eyes. They sniffed the air, catching the scent of prey, and scrambled towards the hillock.

"Oh Goddess Xennia," Arianette whispered, backing away from the edge of the cliff. "What *are* they?"

"They are the Accursed. In the palace, we are safe. They cannot fly, cannot plot or scheme together, and cannot scale the walls. They are mindless. They do nothing besides feed, and destroy, and spread their curse. But the Sky Court extends beyond the walls of the Sky Tower. None of Varik's people on the ground are safe. Every day this horde grows, drawn to the Sky Palace like a magnet. Varik had Anuin and Alarkin, the Earth Lords, carve the pits from the mountain to trap them." Braedin's voice was toneless.

"Why don't you just destroy them?" Arianette asked, aghast. Braedin ground his teeth, his jaw muscles working.

"Varik has forbidden it," he said, and his tone indicated that there was nothing more to say on that matter.

"Well, where did they come from?" Arianette choked out. Braedin and Lorna exchanged uncertain glances.

"They made the first of them during the Culling. But most were created later, as part of our punishment for being on the losing side of the war," Braedon said.

"The Elves were experts at ending us, but we destroy our own people as well. The powerful will always seek to increase their power by marginalizing the weak. Mortal, Fae, Elves, we're all fundamentally alike in that way." There was something in Lorna's tone that struck Arianette as odd.

"I'm not understanding," Arianette said. "Instead of simply destroying their enemies, someone turned them into a mindless flesh craving undead army of immortals? What kind of foul magic is that?" Arianette was appalled, not only by the Accursed themselves, but that someone would tether these poor wretches to the earth like this with no hope of peace or release. It was unnatural.

"It was Elven magic," Lorna said sharply.

"So the Elves used it against the Fae then? But why against the Sky Court? Weren't you their allies?" Arianette asked, confused.

"That's not exactly the way of it," Lorna said carefully. Then she glanced away, not meeting Arianette's eyes.

"The Shadow Court Conjurors stole the Elven magic. The Elves never used this hex against the Fae...not even when it could've saved them from virtual extinction," Braedin said.

Lorna examined her fingernails for a moment, then cast another glance down at the pit.

"We reworked the spells," she said. "The Curse was only supposed to affect the Mortals and the Elves. That was what Ereda said." Lorna's ordinarily high sweet voice was husky with emotion.

Arianette stared at her, eyes widening. She understood now. All the terrible tales told of the Culling, of ferocious Fae with red madness in their eyes gutting Mortals and ripping them limb from limb. *This* was what the survivors who had fled through the Veil had feared. It wasn't just their Fae overlords, who hunted and enslaved them.

It was actual monsters.

"I had no choice. Ereda would have unmade me the instant I dissented," Lorna said.

"It wasn't your fault, Lorna," Braedin assured her, draping an arm over the shadow sorceress's shoulder.

"I didn't know..." Lorna began, but Arianette cut her off.

"You didn't know that creating immortal zombie monsters was an awful idea?"

"You have no right to judge me," Lorna said stiffly, narrowing her eyes. "Ereda told us it would end the war. I was tired of watching our people perish. I didn't know then what a monster my sister was."

"So, you helped create an army of undead immortals to kill my people. Then, when it turned around and bit you in the ass, you stumbled across some prophecy that said *I* was the one who was supposed to break this Curse? And it isn't really a curse at all, is it? It's an Elven spell that *you* stole and *you* cast. And yet you think it's perfectly okay to just kidnap me and drag me across the Veil to clean up your mess? You Fae are even worse than they say," Arianette fumed.

Lorna didn't have time to protest before Arianette stalked off in the palace's direction.

Braedin rushed to her side. "Arianette, wait. I'll fly you back—"

"I'll walk."

"It's a long walk."

"I like long walks," she seethed, barreling ahead up the rocky path.

"Arianette, Lorna didn't cast the spell, she only helped translate –"

"Braedin, I don't care. I'm not interested in listening to excuses." Arianette stomped onward and Braedin continued buzzing around her like a fly she couldn't swat away.

"You know you're exquisite when you're angry." He said it so offhandedly that the words almost didn't register.

"I'm... what?"

Braedin floated down in front of her, blocking her path and forcing her to grind to a halt. She blinked up at him. His amber eyes were luminous and star-touched as he stepped towards her. Arianette smelled the cedar and clove scent of him. She closed her eyes, warding off the pull of magic.

"I said, you are beautiful," he repeated.

Then his lips were on hers. For a moment Arianette swam in the kiss, allowing his soft honeyed tongue to probe her mouth, his hands to rove over her hips.

Then she backed away, shoving him away from her.

"Braedin, I can't do this right now," she muttered, not meeting his eyes.

Braedin hung his head and he looked so sad that for a moment Arianette considered reaching out, pulling him back to her. But he stiffened and the moment was lost.

"Enjoy your walk."

With two beats of his wings he was gone, soaring in the air towards the Sky Palace.

CHAPTER 10

KISS OF FATE

The grueling walk up the uneven terrain was even worse than it looked, but at least keeping her footing distracted Arianette from thinking about that kiss. It had actually been her first kiss. And it hadn't gone quite the way she'd imagined. It wasn't that she didn't like Braedin or find him attractive, it was just terrible timing. And there was the bargain she'd made with his brother to consider.

Not that she thought she was the Legion Queen or anything. That was ridiculous. In fact, everything about this whole bloody situation was absurd. She scowled and kicked rocks as she went, taking her frustration out on the pebbles scattered across her path.

She was hiking up a particularly tough stretch of terrain when she heard a sound that made her blood run cold. One minute the only noise was her own footfalls and the high keening of a falcon overhead. The next, she heard the ghastly crunch of bone grinding against bone, the clattering sound of gnashing teeth, and a low howl that was neither human nor animal.

Arianette froze in her tracks, trying to pinpoint the source of the vocalizations. She had dealt with wolves and wildcats before. A predator was a predator, even if it was an undead Faery. There were only ever two options: fight for flight.

She took stock of her surroundings, dropping into a crouch and keeping her center of gravity low. Ahead of her lay only the twisted rocky path that led to the palace. To her left a copse of tall thin gray barked trees struggled to eke out an existence in the rocky soil. Their silver leaves shivered in the failing light of the gloaming, but she saw no sign of motion beneath their branches. To her right, the sheer cliff face.

Behind her then.

Arianette did not whirl around. She turned slowly, reaching into her leather tunic to remove the bejeweled letter opener she'd carried with her, just in case. One never knew when a knife might come in handy – or something that could pass for one.

They came into sight, two Accursed fairies lumbering towards her. She could almost see what they must've looked like before they were turned. Stringy hair, gone ash grey must have once sparkled as silvery as Varik's. Their ashen skin was perhaps once as bronze as Braedin's. But these were Sky Fae no longer and the hungry grinding of their broken teeth made their intentions clear.

In a fight or flight situation, Arianette's instinct was to flee, but she had to curb that instinct now. If these Accursed still had all the swiftness and preternatural strength of the Fae, there was no way she could outrun them. As they loped towards her with outstretched claws, Arianette wished she would've thought to ask exactly how to unmake, or at least disable, an Accursed.

Most likely an ornamental letter opener was not the best tool for the job.

She dropped even lower to the ground, digging her fingertips into the soil. She could feel the earth around her, the long elaborate root systems of the nearby trees.

She had an idea. One that she was convinced would fail, but was at least an improvement upon brandishing her letter opener. She focused on the trees, the roots, the earth as her mother had taught her to do.

"Mother, if your shade is out there somewhere, lend me your strength now. Xennia help me in my hour of need," Arianette whispered as the Accursed drew near. Frothy red spittle foamed from the mouths of the undead. Arianette closed her eyes.

She willed the trees to come to her aid.

The Accursed were so close that she could smell the sour sweet odor of decay and befouled magic coming off them. Hot tears leapt to her eyes and spilled out from behind her closed lids.

Then she screamed. She screamed at the horror, at the injustice of being here right now. She screamed because she was afraid of dying alone and far from home. She screamed because she missed her dead mother, and because she envied Amabella's power. A proper Wood Witch could save herself right now.

Her eyes flew open as the trees' roots burst forth from the ground. They reached up, up, and out. Arianette watched in wonder, as they grasped the undead Fae, pulling them towards the earth, crushing their bones against the soil.

The Accursed shrieked and struggled to break free from the bindings

The bigger one, the one who looked like he must have been a warrior before he was turned suddenly smoldered, a strange white light engulfing the tattered rags he wore, melting flesh from bone.

Arianette stopped screaming and stared at the burning creature, aghast. Had she done that? She looked down at her hands. They were glowing. Her fingers trailed bright white sparks. But it was not fire. This was something else.

Light, she thought. Before she could consider the meaning of this, or how she had done it, Arianette heard the beating of wings above her. She jerked her head upwards to see him... not Braedin this time. No. This was the Skylord. Graceful as a condor the Skylord swooped in on his crystalline wings. He appraised the situation, the two captive Accursed encased in cages of roots, one set ablaze, bright white flames dancing around Arianette's fingertips.

"I thought you said you had no powers, daughter of the Wood Witch," Varik said in an amused tone as he raised an elegant eyebrow, indicating the Accursed with a cock of his head. Then he reached behind his back, unsheathing his sword and brandishing it at the Accursed. It was ice blue and looked as if it had been chiseled from glacial flows.

As Arianette's attention shifted from the zombies to Varik, the white light on her fingertips sputtered and died. The roots began curling back in on themselves and slipping beneath the surface of the ground as if they had never held the Accursed at all.

The zombies shrieked, freed from their bondage, and rushed straight for Arianette.

Varik raised his sword as the flame engulfed zombie whirled wildly in his direction. With a quick riposte, he sliced the head clean off the creature. Its body collapsed to the ground then exploded into a fine mist of blood red dust. Arianette's mouth contorted into a disgusted grimace as the head rolled across the dirt, landing at her feet, dead red eyes staring sightless up at her. She tore her gaze away from the skull with its blackened skin and focused on Varik again.

His muscles rippled beneath his silks as he swept the gleaming sword in a high arc. The blow hit the other Accursed in the temple, slicing straight through its skull.

It split like a melon.

Then this body, too, exploded into red powder carried away by a soft west wind.

For a moment Varik stood motionless, eyes downcast, focused the spot where the smaller zombie's split head rested on the ground. Then he seemed to remember Arianette and glanced up.

"Do you know that in the Court of Shadows they keep the heads of their enemies as souvenirs?" He laughed a bit shakily as Arianette shuddered.

"Are you all right?" he asked.

She nodded.

"Are you?"

Varik shrugged reaching behind him to slide his sword back into its scabbard.

"Varius" he said, pointing at the scorched head lying at Arianette's feet. "And Rena." He gestured towards the split head at his own feet.

And then it dawned on Arianette why Varik would not simply destroy the Accursed. These nightmarish creatures had once been people Varik had known. Friends, lovers, perhaps even members of his own royal family.

"Were you close to them?" she asked quietly, placing a hand gently on his shoulder.

"It makes no matter," he said, straightening. "Allow me to escort you back to the palace lady Arianette. These paths are not safe for a—" He dropped off before saying Mortal. "Lady to walk alone," he finished.

Arianette was not foolish enough to turn down another offer of an escort.

"It would be an honor to fly with the Skylord," Arianette said with one of her lame attempts at a curtsy. A small smile crossed Varik's lips as he bent and scooped Arianette into his arms.

She wrapped her arms around his neck, her fingers locked in the space between his shoulder blades and his majestic wings. He gripped her to his chest, one hand planted against the small of her back, the other cradling her leather clad legs.

This flight was something different than the perfunctory escort Braedin had provided coming down the mountain. Varik traced lazy circles through the sky, and drew patterns on her back with his fingers, sending shivers down her spine. He seemed in no hurry to reach the castle as his wings stroked the sky, languid.

Suddenly Arianette remembered that first day in the throne room. Varik's breath hot on her neck, his face close to hers. Her pulse quickened and she was certain that Varik must be able to feel her heart pounding against her rib cage, clutched against him as she was.

As they approached the castle he pivoted, banking left so they approached from the rear. Hidden there was a small balcony, a rear entrance to the highest level of the palace that one would never see if they did not know to look for it.

Varik landed and set Arianette down on her feet. They stood side by side looking out over an endless expanse of clouds in every direction.

"Oh." A small gasp escaped Arianette's lips as she took in the view. The balcony was lush with greenery and flowers Arianette had never even seen before, and around them stretched endless sky. They were higher even than the clouds.

"My entire kingdom lays beneath us. To East the Court of Fire, to the West the Sea Court, Shadow to the North, Earth below." Varik said.

"And to the South?" Arianette asked, turning to look out over the southern cloud bank. A shadow fell over Varik's expression.

"That was once the Court of Dreams." He spun Arianette around to face him.

"There is something about you." He raised his hand to her cheek. "That is like a dream," he said.

Then he brushed his lips against hers, so lightly that they barely even made contact. Magic seemed to ripple between them as he pulled away. They stared at one another wide eyed and wordless.

Varik backed up. He opened his mouth, as if to say something, then seemed to think better of it. Instead of speaking, he kissed Arianette again, this time hard and fast. It was a kiss full of yearning and promise.

72

Then he stepped away, stretching his glittering silver wings and vaulting into the sky. His form disappeared in the thick cloud cover.

Arianette stood there on the landing for what felt like a very long time, with her hand pressed to her lips. They still tingled with whatever power had thrummed between Varik and herself during that brief kiss.

The sun set before her eyes, bands of rose gold and azure streaking the indigo horizon. She thought, very far off in the distance, she could see the Skylord's silhouette as he soared above the clouds.

CHAPTER 11

WATCHING AND WAITING

Aciperre perched, hidden, in the turret. It would have been rather rude to impose upon the touching scene beneath him. He watched all the same, not because he was a voyeur, but because that was his mission. As Muírgan's eyes in the Court of Sky, he had seen much today.

He had seen the Wood Witch's daughter command the trees and the golden warrior make a play for her heart. He had also seen the Skylord kiss the girl, had felt the magic course between them. Aciperre remembered what Muírgan had said about star-crossed love being written into Amabella's daughter's celestial destiny. He could see that piece of the prophecy falling into place.

Two brothers , a warrior and a Lord , falling for the same mortal girl . The Goddess had been cruel in arranging that. No good could come of it.

Yet he still could not see how this web that was being spun could help Muírgan's plan come to fruition. What of it, if the girl and the Skylord fell into a doomed affair?

Aciperre didn't like all of this waiting. He wasn't built for it. He was a warrior, not a watcher. If he'd had his way, he would already have led the Elves into battle against the Fae.

Skirmishes at least. Assassinations. At the very least he would have brought the Shadow Empress to heel, the rest of the Courts be damned.

But he would not –could not – defy Muírgan's commands. And Muírgan did not simply want to take down Ereda. Muírgan wanted it all.

And so... Aciperre would watch.

For now.

5

What no one, not even Aciperre had seen was the shadow of Braedin Redwing upon the battlements. He too had been watching Arianette and Varik.

He too had seen them share that kiss.

CHAPTER 12

THE PLAN

Lorna Blackburn fidgeted. She was uncomfortable in Varik's chambers. There had been a time, many years ago, when this had been the only place she wanted to be. Now the large lush chamber filled her with a bittersweet nostalgia that she did not like and was loathe to admit to.

Varik was pacing and his anxious energy was contagious. Lorna might very well scream if he did not stop strutting about back and forth. She had declined a glass of Faery wine, not trusting herself to partake when the two of them were alone together. Now his manic energy was making her wish she had taken him up on the offer. Besides, there was only one person Varik Skyborn was interested in seducing just now. And it was not Lorna.

"She called the trees," Varik insisted for the third time, a gleam in his eyes.

Lorna sighed.

"Perhaps she's just a stronger Wood Witch than we thought. How do we know what a Mortal with the old blood is capable of? Perhaps all the magic in the Ethereal Realms has brought latent powers out. That doesn't mean—" Lorna trailed off. She couldn't believe that she was standing here

76

trying to convince Varik that Arianette was *not* the Legion Queen.

"Lorna, she harnessed pure light energy to set the Accursed aflame. I've never seen anything like it before! If we could nurture her power, grow it –"

"Varik, she's a person not a plant," Lorna pointed out blandly. Varik waved her off, barreling ahead with his newest plot.

"We will hold a feast in honor of our upcoming Soul-fasting at the Court of Fire. Asheron has already agreed, I sent a pixie to him."

Lorna stared at Varik, dumbfounded.

"Your upcoming soul-fasting? You've gone ahead and planned a feast for your soul-fasting? Does Arianette even know that you're to be fasted?" She sounded mildly horrified.

"You heard the geis. Arianette accepted it. If she is the Legion Queen, she must fast to me. And with power like that how can you doubt-"

"Why the Court of Fire?" Lorna interrupted, struggling to keep her tone even. What she wanted to do was rage at Varik. She wanted to tell him, and not for the first time, that he was a self-absorbed narcissist. That she could not think of a worse place in the Realms to hold a feast in honor of their joke of an engagement than the Court of Fire. Except, perhaps, the Court of Shadows.

But she bit her tongue. Lorna knew from experience that coming at Varik with an attack like that rarely resulted in the desired response.

"One." Varik raised a finger. "It is secure. There are no armies haunting Asheron's borders, and no Accursed to waylay arriving guests. He is neutral in the disputes amongst the Courts. Asheron is always neutral."

"He was not neutral during the Great War or the Culling," Lorna pointed out. She waited for Varik to ignore her point. She knew that he would. The Skylord was on a roll.

"Two, Asheron has Elves. They might tell us how to release whatever powers she has."

"A handful of enslaved Elves who cannot even speak their own tongue, let alone translate a prophecy," Lorna countered with a scoff. "Besides, perhaps Arianette's powers will manifest on their own, if she is the Legion Queen. Perhaps we need only wait."

"I don't have time to wait," Varik snapped, picking up a chalice and sipping from it.

You're immortal. You have all the time in the world to wait."

"Not if my head is on one of your sister's iron spikes. The fate of my entire family should have made that clear."

Lorna couldn't argue with that. Ereda had unmade the entire Skyborn line for their opposition during the war. Varik had only survived by being his frivolous impulsive self. He'd been out bedding some solitary Fae trollop against his father's orders when Ereda's shadow guards had infiltrated the palace. Braedin had been out searching for him at their father's command. If they had been in the palace, the Skyborn bloodline might well have been completely stomped out. Just as the Dreamers had.

"No, Lorna. We will not wait around for Ereda to strike first. We're going to the Court of Flames."

"Shall I inform lady Arianette of your impending nuptials and this farce of a celebration?" Lorna asked coldly.

A half smile curled Varik's lip.

"No. I shall do it," he said, tone casual. Too casual. Lorna didn't like his tone one bit. He clearly had some trick up his sleeve. But what could she do? He was the Skylord. She was bound to obey him. They had struck a bargain, a geis of their own. Sanctuary for her within the Sky Court, in return for her help in destroying the Accursed and finding the Legion Queen from the Elven prophecy.

Lorna inclined her head, deferential.

"As you wish. Is there anything else then?" she asked stiffly.

Varik stretched, a languorous feline stretch and Lorna was assaulted by such a traitorous yearning that she had to avert her eyes. He was a selfish arrogant fool, but Goddess was he beautiful.

"Is there anything that I can do for you?" he asked, his voice slippery.

"No," Lorna said sharply. She turned on her heel and stalked from the room, ignoring Varik's laughter as it followed her down the hall.

CHAPTER 13

THE NIGHT GARDEN

The knock came upon Arianette's door as she had known it would. She would not be left alone to sulk forever in her chamber. For a moment, her heart rate sped up at the sound and color rose in her cheeks. She thought of Varik, his silver hair blown back away from his elegant chiseled face. She thought of his breath, cool on her neck.

"Arianette, I wanted to apologize." Lorna's muffled voice came from the other side of the sturdy wooden door. It jarred Arianette out of her imaginings, but she didn't deign to respond.

"May I come in?" Lorna pressed, plaintive.

"It's not warded, if that's what's keeping you from barging in," Arianette grumbled.

Lorna took this as an invitation. The door creaked open and she stood there in her sleek black robes, gold and jet hair knotted at the nape of her neck, peering at Arianette with questioning eyes.

"What do you want?" Arianette snapped.

Lorna took a few steps towards where Arianette sat cross legged on her bed. Arianette didn't miss the look of relief as Lorna crossed the threshold and no surge of magic struck her.

"As I said, I came to apologize," Lorna said, drawing up beside the bed and lighting on it, feet dangling over the side. Her wings trembled slightly and her face was drawn. Arianette suddenly felt sorry for her outburst at the pit. Yes, Lorna had been battling for the wrong side during the war, but she was trying to make amends and fix things.

"Lorna, it's fine. I should apologize too. It's just been... a lot." Arianette said with a weary sigh. Lorna took Arianette's hands into her own and squeezed them.

"You have nothing to be sorry for. It was I who dragged you here. I should have told you the whole truth from the beginning. Then I left you alone out there on the high road, not even thinking – why you could have been killed!" Lorna looked aghast and now it was Arianette's turn to squeeze her hand.

"I don't think this has turned out the way either of us expected it would," Arianette said with a small conciliatory smile. "I know I'm not who you expected me to be. And now I feel like I don't even know who I am."

"Everything moves in accordance with Xennia's plan. You are you, that is enough. Now come with me," Lorna said, hopping off the bed, and tugging at Arianette's hand. "I want to show you something."

Arianette looked a little dubious.

"It's nothing like the pit," Lorna promised. "I just know how much you must enjoy green growing things, living in the Greenwood, being raised by a Wood Witch." Her tone was cajoling as she led Arianette out of her room.

"Where are we going?" Arianette asked as she hurried along behind Lorna. Lorna gave her a secretive smile that said 'you'll see' then led her through an archway in the palace's rear.

Outside the sun had slipped behind the jagged peaks of the mountaintops and the sky was just beginning to darken. They stepped out into a small enclosed courtyard with marble walls that soared nearly twelve feet on either side. Long vines dusted with tiny glowing blooms scaled them. Topiaries carved into the shape of mythical creatures studded manicured flower beds.

"Bioluminescent," Arianette murmured.

"These are the Night Gardens," Lorna explained.

"I've never seen anything like them," Arianette breathed, her eyes darting wildly around the neon gardenscape. Lorna's lips quirked up in amusement.

"Will you be all right right out here? I have some matters to attend to, but I wanted to get you out of that stuffy room first," Lorna said with a wink.

Arianette hadn't yet regained the power of speech. She nodded mutely. The Wood Witch in her, the part of her blood that recognized earth magic, thrummed to life as her eyes wandered the glowing vines and blossoms.

Lorna, appeased by Arianette's enchantment smiled a little. She gave Arianette a small curtsy, then turned away, passing back through the archway into the palace.

At first Arianette drifted from one row of blossoms to the next, inspecting and gently touching the luminous leaves and petals. But the draw was too much for her to resist. She wanted to crawl on her hands and knees, sift the strange gray soil through her fingers to feel its consistency.

What insects might frolic beneath the surface? What other life was buried here? Every growing thing supported other life; it was all part of an extensive network. She knew this from her mother Amabella's lessons. There was an intrinsic connection between all living things.

She tried to shift to her knees but the dress she was wearing was too restrictive. She glanced around. It seemed only the tiny dragonfly-like creatures buzzing from one luminescent bud to another shared the garden with her.

Arianette bit her lip, uncertain. But the pull of the earth was irresistible. She tugged at her dress, shimmying it until her knees were bare. Exhaling, she dropped to her knees. The cool earth soothed her senses as she dug her hands into the soil. It was coarse, a sandy texture that surprised he and explained the unfamiliar plant life. She sifted the grains of sand through her fingers, tilting her head back and closing her eyes, basking in the warmth of the late afternoon sunlight.

As she knelt, head tipped back, she got the strange sensation that she was not alone. The hairs on her neck stood up and her skin tingled. She could sense the soft swell of magic riding the air.

She opened her eyes and found him standing there before her.

Braedin.

"Enjoying the garden?" he asked casually, squatting down to Arianette's eye level.

Arianette nodded, her smile was awkward and crooked. Should she apologize for rebuffing him?

"It is a wonder," she said, running her finger along a trumpeted violet bloom, some sort of lily the size of her fist.

It was firm and velvety and seems to somehow gravitate to her touch.

"What is this one called?" she asked. There was something calming about Braedin's presence, but after that

"Ah, that is a Sky Lily. It grows only in the Sky Court." Braedin said. He picked a blossom and held it out to Arianette.

"May I?" he asked. Arianette nodded and he tucked the bloom behind her ear. The petals tickled her cheek lightly and she stifled a giggle. She reached out to touch another flower, this one a scarlet bud. At the brush of her thumb it burst into bloom, unfurling into a kaleidoscope of vibrant scarlet and gold. Arianette clapped her hands together delighted. This time she did not hold back her laughter, she let it fall like rain as several other flowers unfurled their petals before her eyes.

"Not so beautiful as you, though, lady Arianette. See how the flowers try to compete with you, but you remain the loveliest bloom of all." If someone else had said it, it might've come out as phony or mocking. When Braedin said it, it made her blush.

"You're... wings... are beautiful," she stammered, meaning to trade a compliment for a compliment, certain that she sounded quite the fool. Braedin stretched one muscular wing towards her, an invitation to stroke the tawny feathers. She reached out and gently ran her fingers over the sleek down. This close he smelled earthy and spicy... something like sandalwood and cloves with an underlying sweetness... honeycomb or sweet bark sap.

"What manner of bird do they come from?" Arianette asked, her palms growing sweaty. Braedin tossed her a smile so boyish that it caused a little flutter in her chest. She tried to ignore the sensation rising in her.

"No mere bird, lady Arianette. My wings are of the hippogryph," Braedin said proudly.

"Hippogryph?" Arianette asked.

"It is a creature of myth and legend. A Fae beast with the wings and head of a raptor, the body of a bull, the size of a man. In my father's day they often flew beside us into battle. Once they were plentiful in the lofty peaks of the Sky Court , but now the aeries are empty . Those beasts have flown." He gestured futilely.

Arianette tried to picture a sky full of creatures, half bird and half beast with beautiful banded wings like Braedin's. It was a majestic image. And now they were all gone. Gone where? She wondered. Where would creatures who had called these mountains home for centuries go... and why? Thinking about it made Arianette uneasy.

"And Varik's wings? What fanciful creature do they come from?" She asked trying to change the subject. She realized her mistake as soon as the words left her lip.

Braedin's expression darkened.

"There is no other creature with wings like Varik's," Braedin admitted grudgingly.

"Well, I don't even have wings so," she laughed, awkward, trying to make light of the entire conversation.

Braedin stared at her strangely, as if here searching her with his gaze.

"Are you sure?" he asked, arching a golden eyebrow. Before she could ask what he meant by that, Braedin spread his golden wings and launched himself into the air, leaving her standing alone in the garden.

She stood there for a long while, breathing in the earthy living scent of the gardens, trying to slow her racing heart.

The sun was hanging low in the sky and an evening breeze was stirring.

She might've stood there all evening, waiting to hear what night birds might cry and to see her first fullmoon in this strange enchanted land, had her gaze not snagged on the hawk perched in the poplar tree that towered over the Courtyard. It was a large male, with a bright red tail, a sharp beak, and the most disconcerting sentient yellow eyes. It seemed to watch her, taking in her every motion. She could not shake the feeling that it was not merely a bird. But that made no sense. Surely, even here, a bird was just a bird.

Still, it's penetrating gaze made her uneasy. She headed back to the entrance to the palace, hurrying inside and away from its prying eyes, but not before hearing its high plaintive cry echo across the mountaintops.

CHAPTER 14

AN INVITATION

The invitation appeared upon Arianette's pillow as if by magic. By this point she was not even surprised to see the envelope suddenly spring into being on her pillow before her very eyes. It was pale blue with glittering white whorls and sealed with cerulean wax stamped with spread wings. There was no doubt in her mind where it had come from.

Varik Skyborn.

Her heart beat a little faster as she broke the seal and tore it open, sliding a creamy white piece of vellum from the envelope.

"I cordially invite Arianette Gracelilly," the swirling blue script informed her "to a feast to celebrate our upcoming soul-fasting at the Court of Flames." The broad sweeping strokes of blue ink sent a chill rippling through her.

Arianette stared at the paper, her fury ascending to a fever pitch. Their soul-fasting? When had she agreed to fast herself to him? Their geis went into effect only when it was proven that she was this Legion Queen. Though she'd surprised even herself with it, a little white light and some roots was not solid proof in her book. And at the *Court of Flames?* The Court of Flames had endorsed the council's plan to rid the Ethereal Realms of Mortals . They had kept Mortal and Elven slaves, had fought alongside the Court of Shad-ows in the Great War. She would not feast at the Court of Flames.

Arianette did not bother to change out of her night gown, not having time for the mess of complicated lacings required to don one of Lady Violetta's gowns. She stormed out of her room and stomped up the steps, bare feet cold on the stone floor of the palace. By the time she reached the fifth floor she had to catch her breath. Hiking through the Greenwood was one thing, all the steps in the damnable Sky Court were quite another. She guessed she should be grateful that they bothered with stairs at all, what with everyone around here having wings.

After an arduous climb, she reached the top of the tower. She blew by the guards lining the walls, not even giving them a second glance. They must have been given orders to let her pass, or were none too concerned that a single Mortal girl posed a threat to their Skylord, because they did not stop her.

She burst through the door to Varik's chamber unannounced.

The room was dusky, curtains drawn across the windows. Only two small blue flamed sconces illuminated the chamber. It took Arianette's eyes a moment to adjust. When they did, she saw Varik lounging on a divan. Two fairy women both with streams of blue green hair flowing down their backs and shimmering metallic turquoise scales running from their waists down to their webbed feet, were with him. One sat on his lap, the other had her arms draped over his shoulders, playing with his silver hair.

They were both completely naked. Varik himself was also naked. And glorious.

Arianette swallowed a gasp and quickly averted her eyes.

"I need to speak to you, Varik," she said, voice cracking.

She hoped the Fae women would get the point and make themselves scarce, but they either weren't too quick on the uptake, or weren't interested in her preferences.

"Who is sssssssshe...?" hissed one of the scaled women.

"A Mortal. Or something like one," said Varik. "And one with very poor manners. Tell me, Arianette, do they not knock in Onerth?" Varik inquired, his word slightly slurred. Arianette could feel his eyes rake over her body. She felt naked in her gauzy nightgown. She wanted to turn and flee, but she took a deep breath and steeled herself, standing her ground.

"I'm sorry, *your majesty*," she said, "for the intrusion. But can you explain this to me?"

Arianette held up the envelope.

Her composure was slipping. Seeing Varik with these alluring ethereal creatures filled her with something disconcertingly close to jealousy. Hot tears prickled behind her eyes and she willed them not to fall. He was the Skylord, after all, and she was just a girl. What made her think one brief kiss in the rooftop gardens had meant something to him? What made her think this soul-fasting plan of his was anything more than a power play?

But then she looked up and met his gaze. And there it was; that burning filament between them, that straining energy struggling to connect them, threatening to burn down everything in its path to bring them together. Varik's eyes grew hungry.

He brushed the Faery woman's hand from his shoulder. The other he dumped unceremoniously off his lap. They both squealed.

"Get out," he announced. The two Sea Fae looked sulky as they slithered from the room, shooting Arianette disdainful glances and muttering about Mortals.

"You. Sit," Varik ordered, gesturing to a fluffy blue cushion across from him. Arianette shot him a stubborn look and opened her mouth to protest, but he beseeched her with his enchanting silver cerulean eyes She lowered herself onto the cushion.

"First, what in Xennia's name are you wearing?" Varik smirked, reaching over and pinching one of the night shift's thin silky straps between his thumb and index finger. "You look like one of those whores in that." He indicated the door the Fae women had just slunk out through.

"I thought whorish was your preferred style. Although now I see you prefer your women wearing no clothes at all," Arianette said, folding her arms across her chest.

"I won't stop you, if you'd like to remove that thing to suit my preference," Varik said looking amused. "Have a drink," he suggested, filling a crystal chalice with liquid from a golden decanter set on the table.

"I think not. I'm not here for your revelries. I'm here to talk about this." Arianette held the envelope up again.

"Drink first," Varik said, this time more firm, lacing the words with his magic. The burnt sugar aroma filled the room. Arianette shook her head to clear it.

"I can't drink that. It's Faery wine."

"So it is. And?"

"Mortals go insane when they drink Faery wine."

Varik chuckled.

"Most do recover. Faery wine's reputation is a bit exaggerated." He let out an exasperated sigh. "Arianette, how long do you think you can keep up this charade of Mortality?"

"It's not a charade, Varik," she insisted.

"Prove it. Prove that you're just a girl and this is all a colossal mistake. If you're just the Mortal daughter of a Wood Witch, take the cup and drink the wine. Prove it once and for all. When you recover, I vow to leave you alone... *if* you prove you're Mortal."

He moved towards Arianette, his gaze locked with hers. He pressed the chalice to her lips. Arianette's restraint broke under the weight of his magic. She tilted her head back and drank from the goblet. The wine glistened red as blood on her lips.

Then she waited, defiant, staring at Varik, who appeared quite smug. Because nothing happened. Arianette snatched the goblet from him and took another sip, desperate for oblivion, determined to descend into madness and to prove that she was what she claimed to be. For if she was not, then who was she? What was she?

Varik began to laugh so hard that he nearly fell over. Arianette glared at him.

"What trick of yours is this?" she demanded. Varik coughed and struggled to regain his composure.

"No tricks. It's just as I thought," Varik choked out through his laughter.

"What are you talking about, Varik?" Arianette spoke slowly, glaring at him over the rim of the glass.

"Go ahead." He gave her a small wistful smile. "Have another sip, Arianette." He reclined on his divan, his pale body like something sinuous carved from ivory. "It looks like you're not Mortal after all."

Arianette took another sip, an even longer one this time. Warmth rushed through her. The cloying sweetness of the wine lingered on her tongue. But there was no total oblivion. Escape, it seemed, would not be so simple for her.

"If you were a Mortal," Varik drawled, "you'd be raving mad by now. Trust me, I've seen it and it isn't pretty. No, my beauty, you aren't Mortal."

"What am I then?" Arianette whispered, her voice hoarse.

Varik let out a drunken guffaw then swept off his divan, closing the gap between himself and Arianette. He bent down and drew so close that the pull of his magic became a force of nature. Arianette's skin prickled with goosebumps and her pulse quickened as Varik stared at her. His lips glistened and his blue eyes were bloodshot from partaking in the wine, his violet pupils dilated.

"There is Fae in you, Arianette." He said her name like a prayer, and when he uttered it like that it made her want to believe that it was the only name that had ever been on his lips.

He inched even closer, then froze, his face mere inches from hers. His nostrils flared as he breathed in deeply, smelling the juniper and evergreen that was her scent. Then he pressed his lips to her skin, his mouth gently skimming along her collarbone, then up past the nape of her neck.

"I can smell it, Fae magic, burning just beneath the surface. Hot." He kissed her behind the ear. Arianette trembled. "And fierce. And bright. And so full of light."

92

He reached a hand out and gripped her by the shoulder. Every fiber of Arianette's body screamed to collapse into this embrace, yet she remained motionless as Varik's tongue flicked out, tracing a line from behind her ear to the hollow of her throat.

"But," Varik blurted, "you are also something… other." He breathed the word 'other' into Arianette's mouth, and then they were sharing air, sharing energy. All of her light and heat, all of her otherness, mingled with Varik's cold power of the wind and the sky. Their mingled magic pulsed between them as they kissed, electrifying the very air around them.

When the kiss ended, they were breathless, staring at one another in astonishment. Varik backed away and Arianette had to deny her body's traitorous urge to move with him, to cling to his embrace.

"Stay with me tonight," Varik whispered.

"I can't. I shouldn't." Arianette struggled to keep her breathing even. The entire room was blurring around the edges a bit. Whether it was the potent wine or the magic they'd conjured up between them, she could not be sure, but she felt like she was slipping under water.

She took a deep breath and forced the spell to break, slamming the door to Varik's magic closed with her mind.

"Why are we going to the Court of Flames? And what's this about our 'soul-fasting" she demanded, forcing lucidity upon herself, for the moment, anyway.

Varik groaned and dropped his head into his hands.

"You're such a killjoy, you know that? Must we mix business with pleasure?"

Arianette ignored his complaints and pursed her lips, waiting. She reached for a nearby decanter and refilled her glass. Her hands were shaking, and her nerves were shot. All she wanted was to drown out the questions swirling in her mind. She took a long drink and folded her arms across her chest.

Varik peaked out from behind his fingers and sighed.

"I think Asheron, he's the Fire Lord-"

Arianette shot him a look. She wasn't an idiot. She knew who Asheron was.

"My apologies. Of course, even in Onerth you've heard tales of the mighty Asheron." Varik rolled his eyes. "Anyway, I believe he, or someone in his Court, might know what you are, or be able to figure it out at any rate."

Arianette remained silent, considering this.

"And the soul-fasting," she prompted. Varik shrugged, noncommittal.

"You made the bargain. You agreed to the geis. I recognized your power the moment I laid eyes on you, even if you did not see them in yourself."

This was a fact that Arianette could not argue. She had agreed to the geis, never thinking she really be the Legion Queen.

"Varik, why does finding out 'what I am' matter so much to you? Why do you need me to be this Legion Queen?"

Varik sighed and stretched, indolent, picking up his chalice again and drinking deeply from it. Arianette took another sip of her own, shifting so she sat cross legged on her cushion.

Varik closed his eyes.

"Arianette, you may not believe this, but I truly believe in my heart that you are the Legion Queen who was promised. *From the ashes and the dust, the promised one will come, a lost daughter from the Mortal realm, who is Fae and yet is other.* It's you. It has to be you." His voice was almost reverent as he recited the prophetic verses.

"And if I'm truly not this queen? If you're wrong? Wanting something to be true doesn't make it so," Arianette said. Varik raised his chalice to her in a mock toast.

"Touché, Arianette. But you are the only slight glimmer of hope I have right now." He flashed one of his charming sharp toothed smiles and moved to refill her glass, but Arianette caught his wrist stopping him.

"I think I've had enough," she said. She already felt giddy and a little unsteady. Her hand, with just that touch upon the luminescent skin of Varik's wrist, suddenly ached to wander the curves of his body. She pulled it back, as if burned.

Varik arched an eyebrow and sighed. She did not stop him, this time, when he moved to refill her glass. She sipped the wine in silence.

"Will you come with me? To the Court of Flames? Surely you must be curious, too about who -- and what -- you are."

Curious was not the word she would have chosen. Arianette was terrified. Before she could muster the presence of mind to consider them, words poured out of her mouth. Foolish words. Words that she could not take back.

"Yes, I'll go, Varik. But not for me. I'll go for you. For that last sliver of hope of yours," she said. Then she clasped her hands over her mouth, horrified by her traitorous tongue.

Varik pulled her hands away from her face, kissing each knuckle lightly. Then his lips were on hers again, so hard this time that they were bruising. Without even knowing how she got there, Arianette found herself on her knees. She fell into the kiss as Varik's hands moved over her, stripping her nightgown off over her head, caressing breasts, moving down her belly.

The knock upon the chamber door caught them both off guard.

"Varik?" a voice called.

They both knew whose voice it was.

It was Braedin's.

Frantic, Arianette grabbed for her discarded nightgown and pulled it back over her head. It still didn't look great, her crawling around on the Skylord's floor in a negligee. But it looked a *little* bit better than crawling around stark naked.

Varik shook his head and drew a finger to his lips, hushing her. He got to his feet. For a moment he seemed unsteady, but he composed himself. Scooping Arianette up off the ground, he carried her to his massive bed, where he deposited her tucking the sheets over her to conceal her.

"But the guards, they saw me come in," Arianette hissed.

"They're my guards not his. He may be their commander but I'm their Skylord," Varik whispered back. He kissed her, lightly on the forehead, then took a deep breath.

"What is it?" His voice was sharp and steady. This was a role he was used to playing. The Skylord was a man practiced in both the art of deceit and the art of command.

"Brother, may I come in?"

"No. I'm indisposed with some ladies of the Sea Court. If this is about the trip to the Court of Flames, I have the utmost faith in your ability to arrange everything *without* my help. Lorna can help you. That's what she's here for. Have her conjure up an answer to whatever your problem is."

96

"Well, my lord," Braedin's voice was flat, "Lorna cannot conjure up another Arianette and neither of us can seem to find her."

Varik tensed visibly, but he opened the door wider. Arianette slunk a little deeper beneath the covers.

"What has that to do with me? Do you expect me to lead a search party? I rescued the damsel once when you two fools brought her out to the pits like you were on a rest day picnic. Now it's your turn," Varik snapped.

Braedin flinched at his words.

"I only thought perhaps you had seen her?"

Varik sighed as if his patience were running out.

"I haven't seen the girl since I flew her back from the pits. Something that *you* should've been doing. It was your job to protect her. Instead you left her out there like fodder for the Accursed. You know how dangerous the High Road has become. If I hadn't been heading that way she might be dead right now. And now you've lost her again? Since I made *you* responsible for her I suggest that *you* go find her."

"You're right your majesty, I'll continue to search the castle. I only thought..." Braedin sounded chastened.

A dagger of guilt lanced through Arianette's heart and twisted a little.

"Well you thought wrong. Dismissed, Captain Redwing." The sound of the door banging shut in Braedin's face echoed through the room. Arianette pulled the covers back down to her chin.

Varik poured two more glasses of Faery wine on his way back over to the bed. Then he sat on the bed beside her, handing one to Arianette. She scooted back up amidst the mountain of pillows. Her head was already spinning, the colors of the room whirling, everything sparkling more, and hazy. She took the wine anyway.

"To the small treacheries we commit for love." Varik said softly, raising his glass and chiming it against Arianette's. She blinked at him. Love? Was that what this electrifying connection was? She did not know, but she downed her drink in a single long sip, and dropped the chalice carelessly to the floor.

Varik followed suit. Then, after ripping the covers off of Arianette, he grabbed the collar of her nightgown and tore it in two.

After that... he showed her what real magic was.

CHAPTER 15

A TOUCH OF BLACKBERRY

Lorna glanced up from 'A Brief History of the Dryads', which she'd been quite absorbed in reading, prior to being interrupted by a pounding on her chamber door.

"Come in," she called.

Braedin burst through the door. Lorna glanced at the brooding expression on his face, then wistfully back at her open book. She had a feeling that she would not be getting much more reading done tonight.

"She's with Varik," Braedin declared. Braedin was not prone to outbursts. His half-brother did enough exploding for the two of them. If Varik was a midsummer storm, Braedin was more of an early autumn rain. Gloomy at time, but steady, unwavering. So the intensity of his tone and the nervous energy surprised Lorna.

"How do you know?" she asked, closing the book. She turned her chair to face Braedin and studied him. His face was flushed and there was a wildness in his eyes was unlike him.

"I could smell her all over him. That pine sap and lemongrass scent of hers, that spicy sweet woodsy aroma that plagues even my dreams." He clenched his fists at his sides as he paced with long measured steps back and forth across the room. Lorna worried he might wear a hole in her imported spider silk rug.

"What are you, a poet now, Braedin Redwing? Don't be so dramatic." She rolled her eyes as he collapsed onto her bed.

"I can't help it," Braedin bemoaned. Lorna frowned and knitted her brows. It would appear the little Mortal from across the Veil had charmed *both* the surviving members of the line of Sky with her wiles. Lorna couldn't understand it. Yes, she was lovely, and there was a touch of mystery about her, but honestly...

"You know she is bound to a geis with your brother," Lorna reminded Braedin.

"Not if she isn't the Legion Queen," Braedin countered, sounding a bit defensive.

"If she is not the Queen, she'll be going back to Onerth. Will you follow her there? Shirk your magic and likely die a painful death in Onerth after a few years by her side? Do you think you can just cross the Veil? You'd have to be glamoured, and have your magic bound." As Arianette had been, if Lorna's guess was right. But best not to get into that right now. "Are you that lovesick?"

Braedin grunted and shrugged his broad shoulders, then let them slump. He stared up at the ceiling as if answers might come from above.

Alas, answers rarely came from above.

"Do you think," Braedin asked, directing his attention back to Lorna, "that she is really the Queen from the prophecy?"

Lorna bit her lip and considered her answer before speaking. If the girl truly was in the Skylord's chamber, they would likely be closer to an answer when he'd had his way with her. Varik Skyborn had a way of convincing women to give up all their secrets— and other things as well. But Lorna did not say that.

"I think she is not at all what she seems," Lorna replied instead. "It's late. Why don't you get some rest, Braedin? Hopefully we'll get some answers in the Court of Flames."

Another bad bloody idea, if you asked Lorna.

"Until then, what good will it do to drive yourself mad over it? You and I both know how Varik is with women. If Arianette is with him, why does it even surprise you?" Lorna probed.

"I only thought…" he began then trailed off, but Lorna knew exactly what he thought. He thought perhaps, just this once, he might not come in second to his irascible half-brother, with all his charm and wit and his noble bloodline.

"Get some rest," she urged again. "You'll feel better about things in the morning. Perhaps this is all some passing fancy you made up in your head and Arianette was never with Varik at all."

Braedin rolled his eyes, but he got to his feet and headed for the door.

"Good night, Lorna, and thank you," he said.

Lorna had already opened the tome about the dryads back up. She nodded absently to him. Then, just as he was about to cross the threshold she looked up and said: "it's juniper, by the way."

Braedin turned back around to face her.

"What?"

"That scent of hers that you're so taken by, it isn't lemongrass and pine. It's vetiver and juniper. Perhaps a touch of blackberry."

Braedin groaned.

"Yes. A touch of blackberry," he muttered under his breath.

"It's a very Elven smell," Lorna murmured after Braedin had closed the door behind him.

Then she set aside the book on the dryads, and let her eyes drift over her collection of books and scrolls. She had always been bookish, preferring the study of tomes over performing the blood magic and shadow conjuring her sister Ereda had pressed her to perform. Now, she traced her finger over a collection of bound journals until she found the one she was seeking.

Elven Lore and Bindings the cover read.

Lorna had a feeling this one might come in handy.

CHAPTER 16

THE MORNING AFTER

When Arianette awoke the next morning, Varik was gone. It took a few moments for her to remember where she was. The hazy wine and passion soaked memories of the night before were slow to work their way up to the surface of her bleary mind.

She moaned. Her head was throbbing and her mouth tasted bitter. She glanced around the room for water but found only the dregs of last night's Faery wine in the decanters. Her stomach did a somersault at the smell of it. *That* was the last thing she wanted.

What she wanted to do was crawl back into Varik's big soft bed, breathe in his scent, and sleep off this wretched hangover. But her absence had already been noted. She would have to make a reappearance eventually.

She scanned the room for her clothes and winced as she spied the tattered remains of her nightdress. It wouldn't do to go wandering around the castle in that. She glanced around for something else. Anything else. A blue crushed velvet robe monogrammed with the letter V hung was draped over a chair in one corner of the room.

Arianette snatched it up and put it on. It was way too big, she swam in it, but it smelled of Varik. It disconcerted her that she felt comforted by the scent of his magic. Geis or no geis, she did not want to feel this strange connection to the Skylord that was welling up inside of her. Caring could be dangerous. Especially caring for someone like Varik Skyborn.

She only made it halfway back to her room before she had to stop to rest. It was Lorna who discovered her there, huddling in the fourth story stairwell, clutching her head.

"*Where* have you been?" she demanded. Then she noticed the monogrammed robe and Arianette's condition.

" Ah. I see."

Taking pity on Arianette , Lorna didn't chide or lecture her. Instead , she helped her to her feet and lent her a shoulder to lean on as she escorted her back to her chambers , where she conjured up a bath. Arianette slipped in, letting the scalding water scour her clean.

She had hoped Lorna would disappear by the time she emerged from the water room, but she hadn't. She was waiting by the veranda, gazing out at the distant mountains, as Arianette emerged wrapped in Varik's robe. She cut a disapproving look at Arianette, then went back to staring out the window.

"What?" Arianette asked, defensive.

"You should know that Varik --" Lorna began but Arianette cut her off with a groan as she threw herself down onto the bed and pulled the blankets up to her chin.

"Lorna don't. I already know what you're going to say," Arianette muttered, closing her eyes against the bright light streaming through the windows. "Close those curtains would you?" she complained.

Lorna ignored her request and continued staring out the window.

"Just let me say my piece," she said, her tone conciliatory. Arianette grunted. She deserved this torture.

"Varik has it in him to be an exceptional man, a great ruler, a great mate, but everything that has happened in his life and his Kingdom have made him kind of—" Lorna dropped off and Arianette picked up the thread.

"Messed up. I noticed that, Lorna I'm not stupid. Or blind." *Just terrible at decision making*, she added silently. A curse on Varik Skyborn and his Faery wine.

"All I'm saying is be careful Arianette. You may well wind up soul-fasted to him, thanks to your fool's bargain. So have your fun if you must. Varik is something special, I know. But guard your heart."

There was something in Lorna's tone, something wistful and melancholic. Dawning realization struck Arianette hard as she listened to Lorna's lecture. She gaped at Lorna, at the pained expression on the Shadow sorceress's face.

"You love him," Arianette said softly. Lorna turned to meet her gaze and nodded slowly, her wings twitching.

"Once I did, it is true. Perhaps I still do, in a way. But I stake no claim on Varik Skyborn's heart, and I would not have him back, even if he wanted me. Which he does not." Her voice was matter of fact, but Arianette could sense the pain beneath her words.

It was not jealousy, though. That much was clear. This was just the dull ache of old sorrow mingled with concern. Varik had clearly broken Lorna's heart, and now she worried that he would do the same to her.

"Just be careful, Arianette. He will charm you. He will show you only the side of himself he wants you to see. And you will want to believe every word he says, and so you will. But he was a spoiled, selfish child, and what happened after the Culling left him, I think, broken inside. He doesn't love himself. And so he cannot love anyone else."

Arianette swallowed hard.

"I will be careful," she vowed, though she was not sure she knew how to be careful. Not with Varik. He held an undeniable power over her. Something beyond their control drew them to one another.

"Lorna, what was it that happened after the Culling?" she asked.

Lorna walked over to Arianette's bedside and knelt beside it. She had deep circles under her eyes and her ebony skin looked a bit ashen. She looked as if she hadn't slept at all.

"My sister Ereda murdered The entire royal family. She mounted their heads on iron spikes above the gates of the Sky Tower. They turned every other Sky Fae them could find with a drop of Skyborn blood," Lorna intoned.

Arianette paled. She had a feeling she knew what that meant, but was hoping she was wrong.

"Turned?" she echoed back.

"Into the Accursed."

"Oh," Arianette murmured, not sure what else to say about such unspeakable horror.

Lorna bent then and brushed Arianette's tangled hair from her brow, like a sister might.

Then she grimaced.

"Just one more thing. It's about Braedin. I believe he has a fondness for you. He is a good man. A better man than

Varik, truth be told. If you had not already made that fool's bargain with the Skylord--" Lorna sighed. "But what's done is done. Still, it would probably best if—"

"I'll be discrete. I'll come up with a story for last night," Arianette assured Lorna. She did not want to hear about how Braedin was the better man. She did not want to think about Varik and his dead family. Or about herself and the fact that it seemed she was not who she thought she was. She only wanted to sleep.

"Be wary when you weave tales. Lest you get caught in your own web of deceit," Lorna cautioned. "Rest now. You'll feel better in a few hours. Varik's wine is powerful stuff, Mortal or not."

This was the first allusion Lorna had made to the fact that she too suspected that, after her evening with Varik, Arianette could not be a mere Mortal. Thankfully, she left the potential ramifications of this discovery unspoken.

"A bit more temperance might be wise in the future," Lorna scolded.

Arianette groaned again.

"Lorna, I know."

Lorna chuckled softly, then rose and left the chamber. Outside in the hall, Arianette could hear muffled voices. Lorna explaining to Braedin that Arianette was not feeling well, how delicate the constitutions of Mortals could be, that she was resting and should be fine in a few hours. No, no, nothing serious, just a chill. She would be ready for the trip to the Court of Flames after some bedrest.

And just like that, Arianette remembered the Court of Flames and what she'd agreed to.

A pox on Varik and his Faery wine.

5

Strange dreams haunted Arianette's sleep. Still, when she woke several hours later, she felt better. Not fantastic, but better. And she was famished. The smell of roasting meat and bread was in the air, making her mouth water. So Arianette followed her nose to the main hall where dinner was being served.

Since it was clearly her lucky day, it seemed Braedin was hungry as well. Or had he been hanging out in the kitchens all day under the assumption that everyone needs to eat eventually ? Either way , he was sitting there , staring straight at her as she entered the room.

For a moment Arianette considered fleeing back to her chamber, but her stomach was snarling at her. She needed food. And she would have to face the music sooner or later.

Arianette forced a smile onto her face as she pulled up a chair across the table from him.

"Feeling better?" he asked dryly.

"Yes, thank you. All the excitement finally caught up with me, I suppose," Arianette said, avoiding his gaze by keeping her eyes trained on the array of sugary goodness laid out on the table.

"You know I was worried about you last night. I couldn't find you anywhere in the palace." Braedin was clearly struggling to keep his tone light, but his words came out cold and stiff.

"Lorna told me," she said through a mouth full of sugar wafers. "I apologize. I didn't mean to worry anyone."

"Where in Xennia's name did you disappear to?" he asked, piercing her with his amber gaze. Arianette gave a half shrug, snatching up a honey cake and biting into it.

"The Sky Gardens ," she lied . Lying was an art and unlike Varik she was not practiced in it. But she was not a fool either . If there were one place Braedin might not have thought to look for her, it would be the small garden se- creted away on the topmost level of the castle.

Braedin narrowed his eyes.

"How do you even know about the Sky Gardens?"

"Varik brought me there after the Accursed... thing... he told me I could go there whenever I wanted. You know how I love plants. I'm the daughter of a Wood Witch. I spent my entire life in the forest and the gardens in the Green-wood. I just lost track of time." She shrugged.

"Hmm." Braedin grumbled. Arianette hoped he might put this line of questioning to rest, for both their sakes. Instead he piped back up.

"Arianette, look at me," he said.

She took another bite of honey cake and chewed slowly, looking up to meet his gold flecked gaze.

"Where were you really last night?"

"I told you. The Sky Gardens," she lied a second time, enunciating each word slowly. Braedin sat with his palms pressed flat against the table, as if he would apply pressure until it shattered beneath them. He was so stiff, like a coil wound too tight. He might spring at any moment. Arianette reached across the table, taking his broad calloused hand in hers, and squeezed it. His skin beneath her touch was cool and dry. No magic bled off of him. He was a study in control. He was a rock, a pillar. He was everything that Varik was not. No two men could be any different.

And yet, she thought, *they are half-brothers*. Some of the same blood, that doomed blood, ran through the veins of both Fae men.

"Hey," Arianette said, "there's nothing to worry about. I just caught a chill out in the gardens." She tried for her most reassuring smile.

It seemed to help. Braedin's lips quirked up into a half smile and Arianette breathed a sigh of relief as she noticed some of the tension draining out of him.

"There's always *something* to worry about," he said with a wink and a laugh.

"Well, there's the Court of Flames," Arianette suggested.

Braedin nodded at this.

"Ah yes, my brother in his infinite wisdom, whisking you across half of the Ethereal Realms to parade you around like a feather in his cap. That is a cause for some concern." Arianette quickly diverted the trajectory of this discussion.

"So, when do leave for the Court of Flames anyway?" she asked.

The look in Braedin's eyes made it clear she would not like what he had to say.

"Well, the feast is in five days' time. And it's a day's trip to the Court of Flames." He stalled. Arianette shot him an impatient look. "The day after tomorrow," he finished.

Arianette's jaw snapped closed on the cookie she was eating. She bit her tongue so hard tears came to her eyes.

It would seem Varik didn't want to give her time to change her mind about their late night agreement.

CHAPTER 17

A CALL TO ARMS

"I would know your plan," Aciperre said firmly. He was in his Elven form, free of his familiar's hollow bones and feathers for the first time in a long while. He stood with Muírgan beside the divining pool in what had once been the Courtyard of the Dreamer's Crystal Palace.

Muírgan dipped her hand into the water, swirling her fingers in a slow circle. When she removed her hand, hundreds of droplets separated from the glassy surface of the pool. They spun in the air, merging and separating, forming intricate patterns.

Aciperre gestured. A rune at his wrist pulsed and the droplets dispersed, collapsing back into the pool in a rainbow shower. Muírgan turned to scowl at him.

"Muírgan. I have followed you blind for long enough. I would know how you plan to reclaim the Ethereal Realms for the Elves, or I shall take those who would support me, and try it my way," Aciperre said.

Muírgan studied him for a few moments, then sighed.

"Words, Aciperre, are given life when we speak them. When you utter a word, you release it into the world and it becomes a powerful thing. I was not prepared to manifest my plans with my words-"

Aciperre opened his mouth to argue, but Muírgan drew a sharp nailed finger to her lips and gestured at him. His eyes bulged as the flesh of his lips peeled back and folded over sealing his mouth shut.

"Do not," Muírgan said icily, "interrupt me. Now, as I was saying, I was not ready. Until now. The news you have brought from the Court of Sky proves that all is going as I had hoped it would. So you will hear my plans. All will hear my plans. Gather my Lost Folk to me around my throne," Muírgan ordered. She waved her hand in Aciperre's direction and the skin of his lips split open.

His mouth, which was red and raw, set in a grimace. Muírgan could feel the fury beating off him, the barely repressed rage. But he would not act on it, no matter how much he wanted to. He was a warrior, oh yes, but he still lacked the power and will to defy her.

So, Aciperre did as he was bidden. He raised his hand and the shadow of a falcon slipped inside him once more. He became one with his familiar and took to the skies, uttering sharp high pitched cries.

A short while later, the falcon that was Aciperre perched in the Heart of the Forest. Its great boughs sheltered the throne of iron and ash. As Muírgan approached he lighted from the tree, slipped out of his avian form, and stood beside her at her right hand side. He was resplendent in his Elven armor, his yew longbow strapped to back. He looked the part of warrior as always. But still his lips bled. *Good*, Muírgan thought. Perhaps that would compel him to keep his birdbrained thoughts to himself for a change.

The lost folk crowded around their secret Queen; all the Elves in the broken lands. Some wore their Elven skins, but most were still in the hides, feathers, and fangs of their familiars.

So few. Muírgan thought. Once the Elves had ruled an empire, their people and their rule spanning the breadth of the Realms. Now, they had been reduced to this handful, this few hundred Elves afraid to slip their animal skins and reveal their true forms even here.

"My people," Muírgan began. "The time is coming when once again you will be asked to take up arms. I know that we who remain are but a few, but each of us has it within us to bend the will of the world... together, we might burn the Courts and reincarnate the world that once was." Muírgan's eyes drifted over the crowd, trying to assess how the people were receiving this speech. She was unsure. There was excitement rippling through the crowd, but also trepidation.

She went on.

"The question is: will you stand and fight? Or will you remain here, lost and forgotten?"

There were murmurings from the crowd of Elves and Solitaries. For a moment, she thought they would not stand; that they were too beaten down and fearful to face the wrath of the Fae Courts again.

Then one slender Elf stepped forward.

"For my father, and my mother, who perished in the Culling, I will stand and fight," he said, unsheathing his Elven blade and brandishing it.

Another Elf, a wispy golden haired woman, followed his lead. She slipped her long bow from her shoulder and raised it high above her head.

"For my mother, who remains a slave in the Shadow Court even now, I will stand beside you," she declared.

After that others followed. They slipped the skins of their familiars, raised their bows and blades, and took up the call to arms.

"Burn the Courts!" they shouted.

And Muírgan smiled.

CHAPTER 18

THE JOURNEY

The entire palace was in a state of frenzy the morning they were to leave for the Court of Flames. Arianette had not even realized there were so many Fae *in* the palace. Everywhere she looked Fae servants scampered hither and thither hauling trunks, reading off lists, hustling to and fro with supplies. She tagged along behind Lorna, trying to keep out of the way. Together they darted and dodged through the palace, emerging in the rear courtyard. What greeted their eyes was a veritable caravan of coaches and carts all pulled by...

"Pegasus," Arianette breathed, her eyes wide with wonder. Their silvery manes were braided with bells, their wings white as angels.

"How did you think we would get there?" Lorna grinned and took Arianette by the arm, pulling her towards a coach at the front of the caravan.

"May I, Lady Arianette?" a voice asked as they approached a splendid carriage draped in silver and blue silks.

Braedin appeared before them, swooping in to hold the door to the coach open. He spread his wings regally out behind him and he wore a silver and blue military uniform with wing shaped pauldrons and a wing tipped helm. His antlers extended from the helm, painted in the colors of the Court of Sky as well.

Before he could take Arianette's hand and help her into the carriage, though, Varik appeared at her other side. His silver hair was tied back with a leather thong and his blue eyes sparkled.

"My lady," he said, coming up behind Arianette. She squealed with surprise as Varik lifted her from the waist, twirled her around once, and then set her down in the coach.

A cloud passed over Braedin's expression, and he glanced pointedly at Lorna, who only shrugged. The two of them slid into the carriage, seated beside one another, across from Varik and Arianette.

Arianette grabbed Varik's arm and clung to him as the coach lurched into the air.

"Don't count on him to save you if this coach falls out of the sky. He'll be too busy saving his own hide," Braedin muttered under his breath. Arianette blinked at him, startled by his acidic tongue. Varik only arched an elegant brow at his brother.

Lorna threw an elbow hard into Braedin's rib cage. He grunted in response. Feeling awkward, Arianette relinquished her grip on Varik's arm.

"You're always such a barrel of laughs, brother," Varik said. He pulled a flask from the pocket of his sky blue doublet and took a swig from it.

"For your nerves?" he offered it to Arianette.

"I'll pass," she said. The morning after their night of debauchery was still a little too fresh in her mind.

"You might lay off the wine, brother. It's barely dawn. Unless want every Faery between here and the Court of Flames to know what a drunkard and a –"

"Knock it off," Lorna chastised. "Can we please behave like adults? Give me that flask" she snapped, extending a hand.

Varik narrowed his eyes at her as if he expected her to pour the wine out the window of the coach, but he placed the flask in her outstretched palm. Lorna accepted it and everyone else in the coach watched, alarmed, as she took a huge swallow from the flask.

"What?" she asked, feigning innocence. "You two are enough to drive anyone to drink." She shot a look between Varik and Braedin. The mood lightened after that, and even Braedin took a quick swig from the flask.

This was the first time Arianette had ventured outside the walls of the Sky Tower since she'd come to the Ethereal Realms. Well, except that trip to the pit, which hardly counted. The lands surrounding the Sky Tower were rugged and beautiful. Heather strewn highlands with gleaming chalcedony rock formations eventually gave way to pine barrens; scrub pines and red cedar stretching as far as the eye could see.

Arianette watched the scenery pass by, content with the way Varik's hand rested casually on her thigh. Lorna kept Braedin occupied discussing matters of state and everything seemed to be going smoothly.

Until they heard a Pegasus scream and the coach jerked. Arianette lurched forward, and Varik thrust his arm out to stop her from tumbling to the floor.

"What's happening?" Arianette asked, clutching Varik's arm so hard that her grip left bruises.

Varik patted her shoulder absently, frowning.

"I'm sure it's nothing," he said, though he did not sound convinced. He leaned out over the side of the coach and peered down at the forest floor.

Beneath them a hoard of several hundred Accursed had amassed. They stretched their gangly arms upwards, blood red eyes fixed hungrily on the caravan as they gnashed their teeth. Lorna grabbed Varik and yanked him roughly back inside.

"Are you drunk or just a fool?" she demanded. Varik's lips curled into a grin.

"Usually a bit of both," he said. "A horde this size... someone must be driving it," Varik said, thoughtful.

"Oh come off it, Varik. If her sister were using this horde as subterfuge for an attack we'd already have Elven iron through our gullets," Braedin said, combative again. He too was gazing down at the undead army below, but keeping himself well protected by the walls of the carriage.

Lorna looked uncertain as her eyes scanned the forest rolling out below them. She probed the treetops seeking any sign of Shadow Fae who might orchestrate an attack. She saw nothing until the arrow whispered past her ear, so close that it split hairs upon her head.

"Varik, get down," she cried, whirling to face the Skylord in time to see him raise his hand almost casually. A wall of solid air sprung between him and the arrowhead, stopping the weapon's trajectory. It hovered in midair for a breathless moment. Then Varik blew upon it and the iron tipped arrow shuddered and spun around, cutting across the sky towards the treetops. It found its mark and an archer toppled from the boughs of a nearby sentinel tree.

Then all hell broke loose.

As the body fell from the canopy, the mob of Accursed followed it with their hungry eyes. They scrambled towards it on decaying limbs. As the undead converged on the body of the archer, a hail of arrows rained down from the surrounding treetops. There was a shout as the driver of their coach took an arrow through the shoulder. Arianette screamed as his blood splashed across her bodice. Varik and Braedin both stood and drew their swords.

"Brother, you dare not -" Braedin began, but Varik paid him no heed.

"Do not tell me what I dare. We are under attack. I am the Skylord. It is my duty to lead these men."

"I am the Captain of the Skyguard, it is my duty to protect you."

"Protect the girl instead," Varik snarled. Then he leapt from the coach, his silver wings flashing as he entered the fray.

"Get her to safety," Braedin said to Lorna, his own voice commanding.

"Where are you going?" Lorna asked, her voice shrill.

"To do my duty," Braedin replied through clenched teeth. Then he, too, vaulted from the coach out into the gloaming and the screams of the dying.

Lorna turned her attention to Arianette, who was trembling, cradling her head in her hands.

"It's all right," Lorna said, trying to keep her tone even. "It is probably only solitaries. Varik and Braedin will have done with them soon."

Lorna was lying. This was no ragtag group of solitary Fae leading this assault. This was organized. Planned. Solitaries did not drive packs of Accursed or have access to Elven iron. But Arianette didn't need to know that. It would be easier for them to escape if the girl was not in an absolute panic.

Arianette only whimpered in response to Lorna's attempt at consolation.

"Arianette," Lorna began, taking her face in her hands and turning it up so their eyes met. "I will get us out of here, but I need you to trust me. Do you trust me, Arianette?"

Arianette looked unsure for a moment, then nodded slowly.

"Wha—what are you going to do?" she hiccupped through her tears.

"Give me your hands," Lorna said and Arianette did, placing her hands in Lorna's.

Lorna chanted in the sibilant tongue of shadows under her breath. The tattooed runes around her wrists shimmered.

And then... both she and Arianette disappeared into thin air.

120

CHAPTER 19

THE AFTERMATH

They reappeared, still holding fast to one another, in the cavernous mouth of a cave chiseled into the bluffs just north of the attack. Outside, the din of battle could still be heard, but it was distant now. Out there somewhere Varik, Braedin, and the Skyguard battled the archers and the undead.

"Still think it's a creepy trick?" Lorna asked with a wry smile. Arianette took a ragged breath and shook her head.

"No. I think it's a wonderful trick," she replied.

"Well, here is another one."

Lorna began chanting again. Her dark eyes rolled up in her head until only the whites were visible. Suddenly shadows billowed out from the depths of the cave, coalescing around the mouth and obscuring it. When she stopped chanting she looked drained, as if she'd aged years within a moment.

"The cloak of shadows will hide us. Can you ward it, as well? No such thing as too much protection," she said, pulling a wickedly serrated dagger from her belt.

"My wards will keep no one out. They might startle, but they won't do any real harm."

"It can't hurt," Lorna said. And at least setting the wards would distract Arianette from the battle outside.

Though still shaking, Arianette nodded her acceptance and took the blade from Lorna. She knelt on the rough granite of the cave floor and began scratching the warding runes her mother had taught her into it. There was a brief flash of light as the runes activated, but Lorna's shadows quickly swallowed it up.

"Good girl. Now stay put. You'll be safe here," Lorna said.

"You're not leaving?" Arianette asked, pure panic written on her face.

"I'm going to find Varik and Braedin," Lorna said.

She walked to the mouth of the cave and stretched her membranous black wings. Before she took off she examined the shimmering runes Arianette had etched into the cave wall. They glowed, plain as day against her shadow shroud.

And now Lorna knew why they had looked so familiar when Arianette had caught her off guard with them that first day in the Sky Court.

Because they were Elven.

Whoever Arianette's mother had been, she had been more than a Wood Witch. She had taught her daughter Elven magic. And outside the stolen knowledge of the Court of Shadows, the only people who knew Elven magic were the Elves.

5

After Lorna was gone, Arianette laid down upon the floor of the cave for what felt like a very long time. She was beginning to think no one was coming back for her, that she was going to die in this cave, when she at last heard the sizzle and pop of her wards being breached. She looked up, terrified that it might be an enemy who had discovered her hiding place.

It was not an enemy.

It was Varik.

The sunset bathed his form in scarlet light. His fine clothes were tattered, his moonstone face splashed with blood. His shirt had been torn away and the alabaster flesh of his chest had been raked with slashes, whether from claws or blades, it was difficult to say. Even his silver blue wings were splashed with gore and one hung at an odd angle.

"Varik," Arianette breathed.

"Lorna told me I would find you here," he said. He was wild eyed, his breathing labored.

"You're hurt," Arianette said leaping to her feet and rushing towards him.

"Scratches," Varik said, though he winced as he stepped into Arianette's embrace.

"I was afraid," he said "I'd lost you. When I saw Braedin, then Lorna, but not you." The Skylord was actually trembling, though whether from emotion, adrenaline, or the pain of his wounds it was hard to say.

"Varik, it's all right. I'm fine. What's happened to the others? Where are Lorna and Braedin? Are they all right? Who was it that attacked us –?"

Arianette unleashed a battery of questions. Instead of answering, a sudden flicker of rage lit Varik's blue eyes, silencing her.

"I told Braedin to stay with you, to protect you. And he flew off into the fray. For what? For glory? A obedient captain *obeys his Lord's orders*," Varik snarled.

"Oh, no Varik, I'm sure he—" Arianette began, but the look in Varik's eyes silenced her protests. He wore an expression torn between fury and desire.

"Varik," she breathed.

He silenced her words with a kiss.

It was nothing like the carefree fevered kisses they had shared on that intoxicated night in Varik's bedroom. This kiss was hard and fast, almost possessive. Impossible to break away from. Varik caught Arianette's lip gently between his teeth and slowly pushed her backwards with his body, until she hit the cave wall. He grabbed her by the wrists with one hand, raising her arms above her head, pinning them against the wall. His hips ground against hers as he buried his face in the tangles of her red hair.

"Varik," Arianette moaned his name again but still could conjure up no other words. Instead she pressed her mouth to his, while his free hand slid upwards across her ribcage.

They were so engrossed in the moment that they failed to notice the sizzle of Arianette's wards being disarmed.

"Well. I see you're both alive and well." Braedin's voice was caustic. Arianette flinched at the sound and moved to step away from Varik. Varik released her wrists and turned slowly to face his half-brother, the passion gone from his eyes, replaced by an icy rage.

"Ah. My faithful brother and captain shows up at last," Varik drawled, striding towards his brother.

"Did I not order you to stay with Arianette and protect her?" he demanded. Around him, wind was swirling,

124

blowing his blood soaked hair back from his face. Braedin assessed his brother for a moment, grinding his teeth, jaw muscles working to contain his anger.

"Spare me Varik. I saw her to safety with Lorna. She had a Shadow veil and her own warding spells. She was in no danger."

Varik charged towards the mouth of the cave, snapping his wings open. The full extent of the damage from the battle was visible. Even Braedin sucked his breath in at the sight, while a small sob escaped Arianette's lips.

"When I give you an order, you are to obey it. Day in and day out you remind me how irresponsible, how undependable I am, how I need to 'rise to my station' and 'take control of my destiny.' Yet, today, I give you an order and you disregard it? If you will not honor my commands, how are you fit to lead my army?" Varik still kept his crystalline wings stretched wide, and now Braedin snapped out his tawny feathered crimson splashed wings as well.

"Oh, come off it. Did it occur to you that maybe you should have been protecting her yourself? You had no business taking part in that scuffle. If the Accursed had killed you the Sky Court would have been left leaderless. The other Fae Lords would never support my half-blooded claim. But, of course, taking care of someone else is too much responsibility for the *Skylord*. You can't be responsible for someone else. You can't even be responsible for yourself. You always need a fall man to take the blame if everything doesn't go exactly according to plan. If you care so much about Arianette, then why were off drinking wine with a half dozen Fire Fae trollops last –?"

Varik's movement was smooth as molten steel as he bridged the distance between himself and Braedin. He struck his half-brother hard across the mouth with the back of his hand. Braedin's hand fell to his sword belt, a ferocious growl emerging from his throat. He stopped and did not draw the blade, but his whole body trembled with the will exerted to stay his hand.

"From now on I will lead my army," Varik growled.

Braedin let out a bitter burst of laughter at that. He glared at his half-brother with narrowed accusing eyes.

"Oh, I see now. You want to impress the girl so you're going to rush out and lead an army like you're some kind of hero? Face it. Varik, you're a coward and a –"

"Stop it!" Arianette wailed, clasping her hands over her ears. "Stop it both of you!"

Both Varik and Braedin turned to look at her; at her tear stained face, her round pleading jungle green eyes. Even from across the room Braedin could smell that juniper scent of hers wafting off of her.

He took a deep breath, forcing his fury down deep beneath the surface. For a moment the two brothers only stood face to face, wings outstretched, fury and barely restrained magic pouring off them both.

Then Braedin lowered his wings, tucking them at the shoulders, and spoke.

"Your majesty... brother... you have my apologies. I spoke out of turn. I did not mean the things I said here today," Braedin ground out through clenched teeth.

"It seems to me you spoke your true mind," Varik said coldly, running a hand through his silver hair, sticky now with drying blood. "And from now on I will do as you've suggested. I alone will be responsible for Arianette, and for my army. You, Captain Redwing, are dismissed." Varik's eye ticked as he struggled to keep his composure. Wind was kicking up in the cave, magic he couldn't quite keep checked.

"Dismissed?" Braedin repeated toneless.

"You heard me, Braedin. You're dismissed," Varik repeated.

"From the guard or—" Braedin's voice dropped off as if he were choking on the words.

"From the guard, from my service, from my Court," Varik said, with a wave of his hand.

A powerful wind stirred within the cave.

"Braedin Redwing, I hereby banish you from the Sky Court," he concluded.

For a moment it seemed Braedin would protest, would plead with Varik not to do this thing. They were, after all, the only family they had left. But then an frostiness glazed over his expression. He removed the crest pinned to his tunic, the spread wing emblem of the Sky Court, and flung it on the ground at Varik's feet.

"Arianette," he said "it was an honor and a pleasure to serve you. I'm sorry that the Skylord found my service lacking," Braedin said, his voice low and sad. "Know that I would have cared for you as he will never have the heart to," he added with a sneer.

"Braedin, wait. Varik, don't do this, please," Arianette beseeched them both. She rushed forward, placing herself between the two brothers.

"It is already done," Braedin said. Pivoting, he strode past his half-brother, the Skylord, who watched him walk away with feigned indifference.

"Thank you for your service," Varik said, his voice acidic as he lowered his tattered wings.

Braedin spat at Varik's feet. Then he took to the air without a backwards glance, heading for other skies than these.

Arianette turned back around to face Varik.

"You're not going to stop him?"

"No."

"Where will he go?" she asked, watching his silhouette recede on the horizon.

"I do not know." Varik lowered himself to the cold ground and sat, cradling his head in his hands. "Perhaps the Sea Court. They are warlike and are always in need of military commanders." The anger was gone from his voice now and it broke with emotion on the words.

"Varik you cannot let him go," Arianette insisted. "This is foolishness. I never meant to come between the two of you. Please, Varik, summon him back," Arianette pleaded. The Skylord only shook his head.

"He would not come back now, even if I pleaded with him. I've wounded his precious pride. And for Braedin there is no worse insult than one to his pride. This is not your fault, Arianette. It has been a long time coming. Whatever bond was between us, though, it has been broken. Braedin released himself from it the moment he removed his sigil." Varik picked up the tiny spread wings emblem and fingered it, looking lost.

They were silent for a moment, Arianette gazing out at the empty sky, Varik cradling his head in his hands, until there was a sizzle and pop from Arianette's wards. Lorna's form materialized from the shadows inside the cave, the reins of a terrified Pegasus held in her small hands. The beast rolled its eyes until the whites showed, pawing at the floor. It seemed no less disturbed by Lorna's shadowy teleportation methods than Arianette had been.

"Where is Braedin?" Lorna asked, glancing around the cave. Her face paled as she took in Braedin's absence, Varik's crumpled form, and the tense, melancholic atmosphere in the cave.

Varik and Arianette exchanged a glance. He shook his head almost imperceptibly. Then he sighed.

"My brother is fine, but won't be joining us," he said, forcing calm into his voice. "How many men have we lost?" Varik asked, brusque. Lorna's pale deepened until she looked almost ashen.

"Five and twenty unmade. More turned, perhaps forty. We did what we could to send as many as we could to the Void, but with a mob that size..." Lorna trailed off with a sigh, but the implications were obvious. More members of Varik's Court had become Accursed. More mindless tortured ghouls to stand with Ereda's undead army.

"Varik, the survivors are already en route to the Palace of Flames. We should join them and speak to Asheron about what happened here." Varik nodded with a grimace, rising slowly. He took Arianette's hand and, despite his wounds, led her to the Pegasus and hoisted her onto it, then leapt on behind her.

"I will see you there," Lorna said. Varik nodded and laid his heels into the Pegasus's side.

They took to the skies, Arianette's body pressed against the Skylord's as they headed for the Court of Flames.

CHAPTER 20

NOT SO GRAND ENTRANCES

Their arrival at the palace was not the grand entrance they'd planned. The few sky carriages that had survived the ambush had already limped through the Flaming Gates, well ahead of Varik and Arianette, who were both filthy and bedraggled. Varik, in his tattered shirt, bathed in the blood of his enemies still presented himself like the Lord he was at the gates.

"What, no trumpets? Where's all the fanfare?" he declared, characteristically flippant.

The Courtiers of the Court of Fire clustered around the gates murmuring in low, concerned voices. Suddenly, there was a blinding flash of light. Arianette winced and covered her eyes.

When she opened them, the massive form of a fiery winged Fae blocked gates of the Flame Court. Sparks shot off the massive wings as he folded them behind its back and.

Asheron Drogon, Lord of the Court of Flames, stood before them.

His hair was coal black shot through with bright orange. Tiny sparks danced all around him as if he might erupt into flames at any moment. He was huge, far larger than Varik or even Braedin, and clad all in gold. Golden robes trailed to the floor, an ornate golden diadem studded with massive rubies rested upon his flowing mane.

Asheron ignored Varik, instead raking his molten gold eyes over Arianette's slight form. There was a brief flash of something in Asheron's eyes as he assessed her. It was there and gone so quickly that it was difficult to say exactly what emotion it was that had alighted there. Recognition, perhaps? And something else... fear?

"I was told you were bringing an honored guest. Now your ragtag party arrives at my Court with a Mortal girl in tow? What foolishness is this? Humans are banned from the Realms by the Edict of Culling. You know Ereda and her hoard of Accursed wait only for an excuse to attack you. And so you drag your excuse into my Court, where you know she dare not attack. Seeking what? Protection? Explain this foolishness to me, Lord Skyborn." Asheron's voice was a booming baritone that made Arianette flinch away from him. Varik didn't seem phased by the Flame Lord's blustering.

"Yes, well, I'm certain that Ereda has already trespassed on your lands, Asheron, given the ambush we just barely survived," Varik shot back.

Asheron roared at Varik, who had to dodge aside to avoid a lick of flame spat in his direction.

"The Shadow Empress does not have leave to cross my borders . She would not dare do so without permission , certainly not with her vile undead army," Asheron growled.

"It seems she grows bolder, Asheron. Because I assure you, a mob of Accursed and a band of archers, armed with those foul Elven iron weapons Ereda is so fond of, attacked us. Dozens of my men were cut down and unmade. I can only hope most had passed into the Void before their bodies hit the ground. If not, we've helped bolster the ranks of her Accursed on this day. Ereda herself may not have been there, but her Shadow archers and her undead were."

Asheron prowled back and forth, pacing, flames still dancing around him.

"This is disturbing to hear. I'll set additional patrols, but it does not change the fact that –"

Suddenly the air in the Courtyard darkened and Lorna stepped out of a wavering black slash in the air. A hundred eyes and a hundred arrows trained on her when she reappeared.

She smiled.

"Lord Asheron," she said mildly, dropping into a low elegant curtsy. "It is a pleasure to see you again."

Asheron glowered, first at Lorna, then at his guards.

"Lower your weapons, you damnable fools," he ordered his men. Then he addressed Lorna. "Be careful using those foul shadow tricks in my Court Lorna Blackburn. Someone might mistake you for your sister and put a flaming arrow through your eye."

"I'd like to see them try," Lorna said. She gestured and vanished into thin air, reappearing at Asheron's side. "We came by your invitation, and we bring an *honored guest*. No mere Mortal. Look at her closely. Do you not sense a kinship to her?" Lorna whispered into Asheron's ear.

Asheron snorted, black smoke pouring from his beringed nose.

"I have no kinship with Mortals," Asheron scowled.

132

The whispering in the courtyard rose to a feverish pitch. Arianette wilted beneath the myriad eyes of the Fire Fae. Her cheeks flushed scarlet and she shot Varik a desperate look.

"This is not the time or place for this discussion, Asheron, before all the eyes and ears of your Court." Varik began, interceding on her behalf.

A tremendous crash that sounded like a thunderclap interrupted him. All the light drained from the room. A collective murmur rippled through the crowd as the flickering torches guttered and went out. They were left standing in the deep gloaming. Eyes turned to Lorna, but she appeared just as shocked as everybody else. These shadows were not of her making.

"What is the meaning of this?" Asheron boomed.

Light leached back, and when it had returned, it revealed the black clad form of Shadow Empress Ereda Blackburn. She was tattooed from head to toe in the same strange glyphs that banded Lorna's arms, glimmering on skin the color of smoke. Black smudges clung in the hollows beneath her gleaming onyx eyes.

"You all chatter on and on, and not one kind word about me, as usual." Ereda pursed her thin lips into a frown. "Where is your half-brother Skyborn? Is he not always at your side, guiding and protecting you?" she taunted.

Before Varik could answer, Lorna stepped forward, her violet eyes hard upon her sister.

"Perhaps he's out searching for more of your assassins to run through."

Ereda clutched at her heart, feigning injury.

"You wound me, sister. Everyone here seems so convinced this ambush you speak of was my doing. But what if it was not?"

Ereda seemed to float rather than step forward into the center of the Courtyard.

Asheron flared, sparks shooting off in all directions as he measured his glare on Ereda. All the torches seemed to burn a bit brighter in that moment.

"Who else commands an army of Accursed and Fae archers armed with Elven iron?" Lorna demanded.

"Why, the Elves, of course," Ereda answered, matter of fact. Asheron let out a great guffaw of laughter, though no one else seemed amused.

"The only Elves in the Court of Flames wear shackles and chains." Asheron cut a glance in Arianette's direction and that strange uncertain look was there again for a beat.

"They aren't out leading sorties in my forests," Asheron went on.

"Not all," Ereda looked straight at Arianette, "are in chains," she said. "Honorable people of the Court of Flames," Ereda went on. "You think I'm the enemy, but you are wrong. The enemy walks here, amongst your own."

She pointed a gnarled finger at Arianette.

Ereda opened her mouth to say more, but was buffeted by a blast of wind that drove her to her knees.

"You will not levy false accusations against the woman who will be my soul-fasted mate," Varik declared. He drew his crystal sword from his sheath, towering over Ereda's prone body. Ereda stared up at him, not revealing so much as a glimmer of fear.

134

She cackled as the Skylord loomed, menacing, above her, winds swirling around him. The crowd in the court-yard had grown pensive, murmuring amongst themselves, fearful that a showdown might take place here and now be - tween the Skylord and the Shadow Empress.

"Your soul-fasted mate Lord Skyborn? Is that the way of it? You would wed and bed the enemy?" There was a flash of blinding light as Asheron moved , shoving Varik away from the Shadow Empress.

"ENOUGH! I will not have bloodshed in my halls!" he roared.

Varik stiffened for a moment, then backed up a step, sheathing his sword.

"I will not tolerate Ereda Blackburn 's presence in this Court. She is a murderer, a rogue, and a threat to the peace of the realm," Varik declared.

Asheron sighed.

"Ereda," he said, addressing the Shadow Empress. "It would be best if you would go. This event is in honor of the Sky Court and we all know there is no love lost between your Courts. You have come, you have tweaked Varik's nose. But you were not invited, and I am most displeased to learn your foul army was in my Court. You did not ask leave."

"Asheron, I swear to you, they were not my men," Ereda protested, but Lord Asheron had had enough.

"Ereda Blackburn, leave my Court at once. Take any men who linger in my forests," Asheron thundered.

Ereda slowly picked herself off the ground, dusting off her black robes and looking around at the gathered Courtiers.

"I came here to warn you, you two monumental fools. Don't say that I did not," Ereda said, sullen. Her face looked sunken and haggard but she held her chin high and proud as she gathered the shadows around her... and disappeared.

"She is gone," Lorna whispered. She stared at the place where her sister had been with haunted eyes.

"Lord Varik, you have my sincerest apologies for that interruption. You must be weary from your lengthy journey. Come, Kiriasan will escort you and your party to your quarters so you might rest and refresh yourselves before the Feast tomorrow. We've prepared lodgings for your retainers at the inns in town. I'll have a man show them the way. We can speak more of these matters once things have settled. Kiriasan, show them to their rooms."

As Asheron spoke, a delicate woman with hair the color of sunlight and flames tattooed beneath each eye peeled out of the crowd and appeared before them, bowing.

"Come, my Lords and Ladies," she said.

Kiriasan led them across the Courtyard. Arianette found her short stuttering steps odd. Then she realized why she walked as she did. The woman's feet were fettered. A slave, then. Glancing around the crowd in the Courtyard, Arianette noticed several other men and women with flames tattooed upon their faces and realized the marks were a brand.

She shuddered.

They crossed a drawbridge leading to the castle proper, suspended over a moat filled with lava that roiled and bubbled, bright red and charred black. Arianette edged a little closer to Lorna as they passed over it and through the gatehouse.

Inside, blazing torches cast shadows on the orange and gold mosaic floor. The sound of their footsteps echoed on the tiles as they followed Kiriasan down a narrow corridor off the main hall.

"Will the Lord Redwing be joining you? I prepared for four honored guests."

"My half-brother has other obligations. He won't be joining us," Varik snapped. Lorna and Arianette exchanged uncomfortable looks, but Kiriasan only bowed her head and led them onward.

They were trudging down a corridor when the woman in chains fell to her knees before them. The whole party was forced to jerk to a halt, lest they trip over her.

"Amabella," the woman whispered, lunging forward and grabbing at Arianette's legs. Arianette froze and flinched away, as if stung by her mother's name. For how could an Elven slave in the Court of Fire know the name of the Wood Witch of the Greenwood of Onerth? Unless Amabella, too, had once been to the Palace of Flames.

"I am not Amabella," Arianette whispered, her voice emerging hoarse and shaky.

"Oh Amabella, I knew you lived," the Elven slave persisted. "You've come back for us, at long last!" The woman gazed up at Arianette. She looked neither Fae nor Mortal. She was fair skinned with an ageless ethereal beauty despite her ratty green hair and sunken eyes. Shackled at the wrists and ankles, she wore the telltale flame brands beneath her eyes. Her sharp pointed ears, though, were what caught Arianette's attention.

This slave was Elven.

"They've burned away her runes," Lorna looked like she might be ill as she stared at the angry puckered skin of the slave's arms, chest, and neck. She rubbed her own rune etched wrists.

"Oh my Lords, my ladies. I am so sorry. This one has always been troublesome. Would that she were gone like the rest of her kind." Kiriasan buzzed around, her little bee-like wings fluttering as she shooed the Elven slave away from Arianette. "Tarabelle, leave these royal folk alone and get back to your duties."

"Wait," Arianette said, placing a hand on Kiriasan's arm to prevent her from swatting further at the cowering Elf. "I would have words with her." She sunk down to her knees beside the woman.

"Arianette, we really shouldn't—" Varik began, but Arianette raised a hand to silence him.

"Tarabelle," she said, keeping her voice low. "My name is Arianette Gracelilly. Did you know my mother, Amabella?"

"Amabella, you won the heart of the Lord and you told us you'd be back to free us all. Why did it take you so long?"

The slave collapsed into a sobbing puddle on the floor. For a moment Arianette simply stood rigid, staring down at Tarabelle.

Then she got to her feet and turned slowly to face Lorna and Varik.

"Do you know what she speaks of? This talk of my mother and a Lord?" Lorna and Varik both shook their heads.

"The ramblings of a madwoman, a foul poison tongued Elf," Kiriasan began. This time it was Lorna who interrupted her.

"Enough, Kiriasan. We shall find out, Arianette. After the Feast we'll hold council with Asheron and glean what answers we can from him. If your mother was in the Court of Flames with this woman we will know when and why, and who this Fae lord might be."

139

CHAPTER 21

UNRAVELLING

Muírgan took stock of the unravelling from her throne in the Broken Lands. Though she dared not trespass upon the Fae Courts —not just yet— she had the raven and the hound, the owl and the fox, the hawk and the wolf, all to serve as her eyes. She had never been one to take sides in the Fae conflicts, but she liked to see how the pieces arranged themselves on the board. One never knew what opportunities might present themselves.

Just now, things were becoming interesting.

"Aciperre," Muírgan called, and as ever, the falcon was at her side in an instant. He did not shift back to his Elven form.

"You say the one called Braedin Redwing has flown in disgrace from the Skylord's service?"

Aciperre nodded, his intelligent yellow eyes intent on Muírgan.

"Yes, my queen. After the battle, they quarreled and he flew towards the Court of Sea."

"And they do not know that the attack was at my command?" Muírgan inquired, arching one brow.

"No, my Queen. I used only Solitaries and Undead in the attack. The blame has fallen squarely on the Shadow

Empress Ereda's shoulders." Muírgan smiled at this news. Those short-sighted Fae fools were playing right into her hands.

"Excellent. Find the Redwing boy for me, Aciperre. Bring him here, to the Broken Lands," she ordered the falcon.

Though he had long since grown weary of playing the role of errand boy, Aciperre knew better than to argue with Muírgan. He would not make that mistake again. Not after the last time.

And so, he took to wing, seeking the banished captain of the Sky Guard.

5

It did not take long for Aciperre to track down Braedin Redwing. He discovered him skulking forlornly around the borders of the Sea Court. Aciperre was glad to have caught up with Braedin before he ventured beneath the waves and into Nimione's territory. At his advanced age Aciperre was not at all interested in slipping skins with another familiar. Especially not a sea creature. They were as querulous and temperamental as their Fae masters. The Merfolk and Selkies, always waging war amongst themselves, or with one rival Court or another.

Aciperre circled three times, then landed on a drift wood log near to where the Sky Fae had built a small fire. He was roasting some sea bird he had caught on a spit, a gull most likely. Good riddance. They too were ornery creatures.

Braedin's shoulders were slumped, his wings drawn in close, and he wore melancholic defeat on his face. One might think the whole of the Realms was against him. And perhaps it was. He had gone from leading an army to a solitary Fae warrior wearing no sigil and attempting, in vain it would seem, to beg an audience in the Sea Court. It was certainly not the brilliant Captain Braedin Redwing's shining moment.

Aciperre gestured into the air. The shadow of his falcon peeled away. In its place, a tall sinuous man crouched upon the driftwood log. He wore green leather armor emblazoned with the image of a great golden tree across the breast. His golden cloak billowed in the sea breeze.

"Hail," he called out, rising to take a few careful steps towards the Fae by the fire. "I come with peaceful intentions," he said, palms outstretched to show he wielded no weapon and posed no threat.

Braedin leapt to his feet, placing a hand on the pommel of the sword at his belt. But there was no fight in his eyes. More than anything, he looked bewildered to see this Elf, of all things, approaching him.

"I did not know that there were any of your kind left in the wilds," Braedin said blandly, still fingering his sword belt but making no motion to draw the blade. Aciperre gave a snort of laughter.

"We are few, and most would never dare set foot within the Fae Courts. But I am here on a mission for my Lady. She seeks you, Captain Redwing," Aciperre explained.

"And who might your lady be?" Braedin asked, frowning and narrowing his eyes.

"She calls herself the Queen of Nothing. You, however, are likely more familiar with her name in the Elven histories. Perhaps the Queen Who Wears No Crown rings a bell?"

"The Queen Who Wears No Crown," Braedin repeated. "Muírgan Vivane? Queen of the Elves? But how can that be?

They killed her with all the others when they demolished the Court of Dreams."

Aciperre stared at Braedin with his piercing yellow avian eyes.

"Aye, so they say. Yet they also say that I was killed. Yet here I stand. I, by the way, am Aciperre Ambrosius. You might have heard of me as well."

Aciperre had won more battles during the Great War of the Courts than any other Elven general. All the Fae had once quaked in their boots when his name was uttered. Of course Braedin Redwing would recognize it.

Braedin squinted at Aciperre, uncertain.

"If it's the girl she seeks, if this is about the prophecy, I left her with the Skylord," Braedin said, a touch of ice edging his tone. Aciperre shook his head.

"No. It is you she seeks, Captain Braedin Redwing, Guardian of the Westwood—"

"I am that man no longer," Braedin interrupted, his voice soft and sad.

"All the same, it is you she sent me for, not the girl. Will you take a chance? Seek your fortune in the Broken Lands? Or will you sit here on this lonely beach, feeling quite sorry for yourself, hoping Nimione takes pity on you? In the Court of Sea you would be just another in Nimione's ranks, passing to the Void young, in one of her petty skirmishes or another. My lady would make you a leader amongst the Fae, Elves, and Mortal alike. She seeks to build a new unified Realm and would have you by her side."

Braedin considered Aciperre for a moment, brow furrowed.

"And how do I to know what you say is true? That you won't lead me into some trap when we reach the Broken Lands?" he asked.

Aciperre shrugged.

"I know that trust has been hard fought between our races. But once I stood beside your father on the field of battle. We fought, not only for our own survival, but for what was *right* . Fight beside the Elves , Braedin Redwing . Help us rid the Ethereal Realms of the likes of Ereda Blackburn."

Braedin gazed out at the waves crashing upon the breakwaters in the distance. Then he turned back towards Aciperre.

"All right, Aciperre. I will honor my father's memory. Take me to Muírgan," he said.

CHAPTER 22

ELVEN MAGIC

Muírgan did not receive him at her throne beneath the Heart of the Forest, but staged their first contact beside a small stream that had only recently bubbled up from what had once been lifeless parched earth.

"I am glad that you decided to come," Muírgan said. Braedin nodded to her but it was clear he was on edge. He was the image of tension, standing rigid beside her with his right hand glued to his sword belt. As if Fae arms were a match for Elven magic.

"Do you see this stream, Braedin Redwing?" Muírgan asked. She sat down beside the pristine sweet-smelling waters and let them rush over her fingertips.

Braedin nodded.

"This stream was dry for over a hundred years. Now it runs, clear and true, through these lands once more. We Elves are like this stream. We have been silent, hidden, and dead in the eyes of the Courts for long years. We let the Fae believe that, not only are we no longer a threat, but that we have ceased to exist."

Muírgan paused. Curling one finger, she whispered a command to the waters. They shifted, swirling until the surface of the stream became a whirlpool.

"But we are still here. And we will rise again," she finished. Braedin looked skeptical.

"How?" he asked, narrowing his eyes.

"You believe," Muírgan said, conjuring up a perfect golden rose from thin air and setting it to spinning in the space between herself and Braedin. "That your magic is your own; that it belongs to you. It does not."

Muírgan flicked her finger and the rose exploded into a shower of golden dust.

"All magic belongs to Her. Elven, Mortal, Fae, it does not matter. It is all leant to us by the Great Mother Xennia. Some may have proclivities towards one element, yet we can all use magic, any of it, all of it, for a time. We simply must give of ourselves to do so. You Fae do not recognize this. And that," Muírgan moved her hand ever so slightly so that a ball of pure white light appeared in her palm. She flicked the ball in Braedin's direction and it grew and expand until it seemed it would consume him.

Braedin moved to block the spell but Muírgan raised her hand again and the ball of light vanished.

"...Is why," she picked back up, "your magic is weak. And mine is strong." She curled her lips into a mischievous smile. Braedin eyed her with a mixture of fear and curiosity.

"So did you bring me here to mock me, then?" he asked, twirling his own fingers in the air, spawning a small tornado that danced in his palm. The move was neither threat nor challenge, but a warning. Though her Elven magic may be powerful, he was not at her mercy.

"No," Muírgan said. "I brought you here to teach you." She blew lightly in Braedin's direction and his tiny tornado rose and dispersed itself, carried off by Muírgan's breath. Braedin's eyes widened.

"But why me?" he asked, still unconvinced.

Muírgan laughed and it was the sound of tinkling bells, the sound of falling water, the sound of breaking glass all at once.

"Why not you?" she asked cocking her head to one side and sending spray of hair cascading over her narrow shoulders.

"Lorna would be better suited. She speaks your tongue, understands your magic."

"Braedin," her form blurred as she travelled the space between him and herself in a single blinding motion. "I want to Burn the Courts," she whispered, her mouth so close to his ear that her cool breath made the hairs on the back of his neck stand up.

"Burn... the Courts..?"

Muírgan nodded. This was the delicate part. This was where she would have to be very careful. For Braedin was *of* the Courts. Muírgan was taking a gamble. This man had stood in his younger brother's shadow, despite being the eldest and better fit to rule. This man had watched his arrogant sensualist brother steal the heart of the woman he loved. Then he had been banished and left with nothing. This was a man who might be turned against the hierarchy.

"The Ethereal Realms bleed," she said. "They have bled for thousands of years. My kind have been all but wiped out, the Mortals banished beyond the Veil. Even now, your Skylord conspires with the Lord of Flames to wage war against

147

the Shadow Court, while armies of the undead amass on their borders. Do not forget that the Broken Lands were once the Court of Dreams."

"It was the Elves who destroyed the Court of Dreams," Braedin countered.

"To close the Veil and save the Mortals," Muírgan hissed. "We were fighting for our survival. If the Fae Courts thought the Elves gone, it would give those few who survived time to regroup. That is why we sacrificed ourselves. That is why the Dreamers sacrificed themselves."

"But so few of your people survived. How many? A handful? How do you plan to burn the Courts? You're one woman. No matter how powerful you are, you cannot hope to—"

Muírgan raised a hand and gave a long low whistle.

They melted out of the forest. Winged creatures, four legged creatures, creatures that slithered, creatures that crawled. And one by one, the shadows of their animal forms peeled away and Braedin found himself surrounded by hundreds of the lost ones, the forgotten folk... the Elves.

"We do not wish to annihilate the Fae, as they once tried to do to us. That is not the Elven way. I wish only to unify the Realms in peace, so that the Veil might be lifted and we might all live in harmony again. I would give you power beyond your wildest imaginings. You need only join us in our quest for unity. Will you, Braedin Redwing?"

Braedin looked around at the somber faces surrounding him. These Elves were a people whose long limbed delicate beauty belied a power that made Fae magic look like child's trickery. Power, the one thing never within his grasp

148

in the Sky Court, was being offered to him on a silver platter.

He nodded.

"Come then," Muírgan said.

She led him to a glade, resplendent with wildflowers of every color. The trees surrounding it were still young, fresh growth in the ashes of what had once been.

"Ours is the first magic," Muírgan said. "Old as the skies, deep as the seas. It is *of* the earth not *from* the earth. So we must give of ourselves each time we wield it. The runes tie you to the Great Mother, allowing you to tap deeper into her power."

Muírgan dipped a reed brush into the ceramic pot. She dabbed it to Braedin's chest. It tingled slightly at first, then burned like the sharp nick of a razor where it touched his bronze skin.

"The first Rune I paint all warriors with is Cruciamena, Painbringer, for to live is to suffer, and to tap into that suffering brings substantial power."

Muírgan moved the reed in a slow sweeping motion, causing a line of fire to burn up Braedin's chest. He did not flinch.

"Close your eyes, Braedin Redwing. Focus on your pain, let the ache burn through you. Think about what hurts you most," Muírgan murmured.

And so Braedin did. He thought about Arianette; the clean spicy scent of her. Juniper, vetiver, and blackberry. He thought about that moment by the pit when she had spurned his kiss. He thought about Varik's hand resting on her thigh. The deep jungle that lay within her verdant eyes, and the look in them when she gazed at his half-brother.

He let out an animalistic groan of rage and frustration, and opened his eyes. Muírgan was staring at him, her expression curious.

"You were thinking about the Wood Witch's daughter, were you not?"

Braedin colored slightly but nodded.

"That is good," Muírgan murmured. "Now I shall bind you to her."

She made a series of quick swipes with her brush and murmured something in the meandering tongue of the Elves.

Pain... no, more than pain, sheer agony, lanced through Braedin. For a moment he thought his heart might stop in his chest. When the excruciating sensation passed, he gazed down at the black mark emblazoned upon his chest, and thought of suffering, and Arianette, and juniper, vetiver, a touch of blackberry.

CHAPTER 23

THE RUNE

Arianette dreamt of the strange tree and the burning forest again, just as she had on her first night in the Ethereal Realms. It was much like the first dream, only even more terrifying. She awoke to a burning sensation in her chest that did not pass with the dream. Frantic, she threw the covers off herself, and pressed her hands to the space between her breasts where the sensation was emanating from.

The spot was burning hot, so hot that when Arianette touched it, she hissed and drew her hand back, startled. She traced tentative fingers along what felt like incisions etched into her flesh. She got to her feet, heart beating fast, blood pounding in her temples, and padded across the room to the looking glass mounted on the wall.

Her reflection was as it had always been. Long fiery red hair, verdant green eyes, an eerily pale complexion. But there, dead set in the center of her chest, was a rune reflecting at her. It was a pulsing red and black thing the color of smoldering hot coals. She traced a finger along its lines, panic rising in her throat.

"*Cruciamena,*" the Elven word whispered in the back of her mind, coursed through veins her as she touched the

151

rune. She pulled her hand back from it as if stung. Rushing to her bed, Arianette wrapped the tangled sheet around herself and fled the room.

"Lorna!" she shouted, pounding on the door across the corridor from her own.

Lorna opened the door, yawning and rubbing the sleep from her dark purple eyes.

"Arianette, whatever is the matter?" Lorna asked.

Arianette didn't answer, but pushed past her into the room. Slamming the door behind her, she pressed her back up against it, and stood there panting and wild eyed. Lorna opened her mouth to ask her again what had happened, but the question bubbling up on her lips died when Arianette lowered the sheet, revealing the burning mark.

"Goddess Xennia above us," Lorna breathed, her expression somewhere between fascination and horror.

"What *is* it?" Arianette demanded, her voice coming out strangled.

Lorna reached out to touch the strange marking. She yelped and pulled back her hand, as her fingers grazed it. The skin on her fingertips came away singed. She glanced from her burned fingers to Arianette and cleared her throat.

"Well, it's Elven," she said quietly, bending to study the brand, without touching it this time. "It's a rune called –"

"Cruciamena," they finished in unison. Lorna's eyes widened.

"How could you possibly know that?" she asked.

"I don't know, I mean- I can't explain it. It's as if it *told* me. Cruciamena, what does it mean?" Arianette asked, the timber of her voice growing higher and more desperate.

"It means Painbringer," Lorna said.

Arianette stared at Lorna, her face pale as the bedsheet she was wrapped in. Lorna could tell that her panic was close to breaking free.

"Settle down. It's not as bad as it sounds," she reassured her. "The elves used these runes to-" Lorna dropped off trying to figure out the best way to explain it.

"Well to channel power, to enhance it. Cruciamena does not mean that it will hurt you, despite the name, and what it did to my fingers," Lorna sucked the puckered skin of her burned fingertips. "That is protection to make it harder to remove. This is a rune that gives one the power to channel their own pain and convert it into power." Lorna pulled her robe away from her wrist and revealed a small tattoo, tiny twin to Arianette's.

"See, I wear it too. Though more subtly, I admit." Lorna tried to coax a smile from Arianette. It didn't quite work, but she seemed to relax a little.

"We need to show this to Varik," Lorna said, but Arianette shook her head.

"No," she hissed, snapping the sheet back up to cover the burning mark. "I don't want him to see me this."

It wasn't that she did not want the Skylord's eyes on her body. Varik had seen and touched parts of Arianette that she had not even known existed. But this was different. This rune meant power. Actual power. There was their geis to consider. Something like this might well prove beyond doubt that she was the Legion Queen and end her dreams of returning to the Greenwood forever.

"Please Lorna. Don't tell Varik. At least not yet. Let's figure out what it means first," Arianette pleaded.

Lorna considered her for a moment.

"All right. I suppose we need not tell the Skylord just yet. But there is someone else who does need to know." She paused, looking shrewdly at Arianette.

"I do not want anyone else to know" Arianette whimpered, yanking her robe closed, as if concealing the rune might make it go away.

"It is Asheron I speak of. After our brief discussion with the Elven slave this morning, I believe Asheron knows more than we had originally thought," Lorna explained.

Asheron had scorned and mocked Arianette before his entire Court. She did not want to discuss the rune with Asheron, but she had a feeling Lorna was right. If anyone might have answers to who –and what – she was, and where the rune might have come from it would be Lord Asheron.

CHAPTER 24

FAILED DIVERSIONS

Lorna arranged the meeting and a diversion for Varik, which of course she said nothing about to Arianette. When the clock struck twelve, she rapped on Arianette's door. It cracked open and Arianette slipped out. Lorna took her hand and squeezed it.

"Let's go," she whispered, raising her hand and calling the shadows to her and cloaking them both.

They moved unseen through the corridors of the Palace of Flames. Even without the help of the shadows, they likely would not have been spotted. Everyone was sleeping to prepare for the feast and Lorna had a knack for discovering secrets. She'd known about the palace's hidden passageways for years, and once inside the shadows whispered to her, leading her straight to Asheron's chambers.

The passage led them to a wall with a false back that slid aside with a touch. Not very inventive, but functional enough. The Fire Fae weren't known for their creativity.

Arianette and Lorna stepped into the Fire Lord's chamber. It was opulent, as everything in the palace was. The walls were covered with elaborate red and gold tapestries depicting magnificent battles. In the center of the room, Asheron sat in a large throne-like chair, looking pensive.

"Lady Blackburn," he said, rising. "I'm most curious to know what matter is of such great importance that it warrants this late night tete a tete."

Lorna opened her mouth to answer, but never got the chance. Just then there was a tremendous crash as the doors to Asheron's chamber burst open and a mighty gust of wind rippled through the room.

Varik Skyborn entered, several Fire guards on his tail protesting.

"I, too, am dying to know," the Skylord drawled, stalking into the room. He looked the image of a true lord in his sky blue and silver fighting leathers, his cloak fluttering behind him in the torrent of wind that swirled around him.

"Varik," Lorna breathed. "What are you doing here?"

"You think I'm a complete fool, Lorna. But I'm not. I knew you were up to something when you sent those girls to me. So I dismissed them, and followed you."

"Girls?" Arianette echoed, glancing from Lorna to Varik.

"How did you find—we were shadow cloaked," Lorna stammered.

Varik snorted.

"Do not forget that I am the Skylord, Lorna. I may not always act it, but I have powers you can't even imagine. Your little web of shadows is no deterrent for me."

Lorna paled. She had been a fool to underestimate him. For all of his frivolous ways, royal blood flowed through Varik's veins. He was a formidable force of nature, and though he often played one, clearly not a fool.

"So, if you please, would one of you be kind enough to tell me why my advisor and the woman who has sworn to soul-fast to me, who I have sworn to lay my life down to protect, are here with the Fire Lord behind my back?" His tone was casual, amused even, but his blue eyes were hard.

"I'd be interested to know the same thing," grumbled Asheron. Lorna's heart was up in her throat, pounding too fast. This was not going the way she had intended at all.

Then Arianette stepped out from behind Lorna, standing between her and the two Fae Lords. She pulled aside her white robes. Her hair tumbled in flaming rivulets over her shoulders, covering her bare breasts, and seeming to wreath the mark emblazoned on her alabaster chest. The rune pulsed with power.

Varik sucked his breath in, eyes widening. Asheron only dropped his head, shoulders drooping.

"So, it is as I thought. I knew I recognized Amabella in the girl, but I did not want to believe it," Asheron said, sounding defeated.

Arianette looked at him with wide, luminescent green eyes blurred by the tears welling up behind them.

"What do you know about my mother? And of this rune?" she asked. "Can you tell me what is happening to me?"

For a moment, Asheron only pursed his lips together and it seemed he would not speak. Then he muttered something under his breath and motioned for them to sit.

"I will tell you all that I know," he said, "about this girl who will bring trouble down on all of our heads."

CHAPTER 25

ORIGINS

"Amabella Gracelilly, was a slave in my Court. An Elven slave. Suffice to say I had a fondness for her. She had a child, eight or nine summers at the most at the time of the Culling. Not my child, make no mistake. Amabella was a favorite in my pleasure house amongst all the Fae Lords and nobles. The Dreamers loved her especially. It was the Lord of Dreams who convinced me to release her from bondage when I signed the Pact and the Culling began."

Asheron cleared his throat.

"He and I helped Amabella glamour her child, erasing the girl's memories of The Court of Flames. I arranged to have them both sent to the Court of Dreams. From there they might seek safety in the Mortal realm of Onerth. We all knew that Amabella might well sacrifice her immortality in doing this. Elves cannot thrive in Onerth because of the magic in their blood. But the child, she would be bound, so the Veil would not feed on her magic. The child, at least, would survive, until it was safe to return her to the Ethereal Realms, so long as her magic remained checked."

"So you bound her power, and gave her a Mortal skin to wear," Lorna said softly.

"No one knew that the Elves would bring down the Court of Dreams. We thought there would be some resolution between the Dreamers and the other Courts. There always had been in the past. No one knows what happened in those last hours. Perhaps the Dreamers knew that the Elves plan to seal the Veil would be the end of them all. It would not surprise me. They were always a noble lot."

"Or perhaps they did not, and the Elves tricked them into destroying their own Court," Varik countered.

Asheron levelled his gaze on Varik.

"Perhaps the Elves themselves did not know what would happen. Muírgan was ancient and powerful, but she was not omniscient."

Varik seemed to grow impatient with this line of conversation. He fluttered his wings, which were already beginning to heal, irritably.

"So Amabella was Elven, not a Mortal Wood Witch. But who was Arianette's father?" Varik asked. For just a second a look of terror flashed in Asheron's molten gold eyes. Then it vanished replaced by steel.

"I cannot answer that and it does not matter. He was a Dreamer and the Dreamers are gone," Asheron growled.

Varik changed tact.

"And can you break the bonds on her power? Can you restore her memory and dispel the glamour?" Varik's words ran together, he spoke them so.

Asheron shook his head.

"It is Elven magic, I only helped by lending my power to the conjuring. Amabella crafted the spells. It was a nasty bloody business, too, binding the girl." Asheron paled. His shudder was almost imperceptible. Lorna opened her mouth to interject but Asheron did not let her get far.

"Even if you could somehow break the bonds , Shadow Sorceress, all that power released, all at once... it could destroy the girl. Her mind and body have been Mortal for so long. Moreover , it appears someone , or something , is already unleashing her. That rune... that is Elven work."

"Who, though, and why," Varik wondered, a note of genuine concern in his voice. "The Elves are all dead or enslaved."

"And the enslaved have all had their runes removed. It would be impossible for them to work their magic," Lorna murmured, furrowing her brow.

"Yes, but, there is the prophecy," Varik said.

Arianette groaned, cradling her head in her hands. It all came back to this Prophecy again. Asheron only let out a great bellow of laughter.

"Oh I see now, Skylord. You believe she is the Legion Queen. That is why you want to soul-fast yourself to her. Now it all comes together."

Varik's temper flared and the air swirled around him again, rising with his emotions.

"Don't presume to know my reasons, Asheron Drogon," he snarled, placing a protective hand on Arianette's shoulder.

"You know what she is, I see it in your eyes. You cannot fail to see that she is the prophecy made manifest. Help us keep her safe, ally with us against Ereda. Vow to it. Right here and now. She is the one who would come to unify the realm and protect it from Ereda's reign of darkness."

"I'm not, I'm just—" Arianette protested feebly. But the burning mark on her chest throbbed and she realized that she did not know who or what she was. She went silent and it was Asheron who spoke again.

"Elven prophecies are notoriously vague, complex, and often prove false, Lord Skyborn. Ereda has left my lands unmolested for years. Why should I risk my people's safety and let war in through my front gates for the sake of the Sky Court?" Asheron demanded.

"If the Sky Court falls, Ereda and her army of Accursed will be on your doorstep. The Court of Flames could be the next to fall to her," Varik said.

"Now it is you who makes assumptions, Skylord. Ereda has never harried my borders with her armies. She seeks to assault the Sky Court because it is weak, run by a spoiled self-absorbed Lordling, all but leaderless," Asheron accused, rising and prowling around Varik, red and white flames shooting off of his golden armor.

Varik got to his feet, air still eddying as he struggled to maintain his composure.

"She has already ventured onto your land without your leave. She grows bolder," Varik ground out.

"They were on my land to ambush *your* caravan," Asheron pointed out with a swipe of his hand in Varik's direction. Lorna moved between the two Fae Lords.

"Asheron, I know my sister. She will not be content with conquering the Sky Court. And if she believes Arianette is the Legion Queen, which I think she does, she will stop at nothing to destroy her and us out of pure jealousy and spite. Then, once she has conquered the kingdom of Sky she will set her sights elsewhere. The Court of Flames, the Sea Court… perhaps she'll cross the Veil and take Onerth, if she can. Ereda needs to be stopped."

"Would that this prophecy did not exist," Arianette's burst out, startling them all. Varik stroked her shoulder.

"It will be all right, Arianette. If he won't ally with us of his own accord, I propose a Reckoning," Varik declared.

All eyes turned to him.

"I will not be known as the Lord who called down the Reckoning over a half-Elven mongrel and some ink upon a page," Asheron decreed.

"But I will be," Varik said. He was standing straight and tall, eyes crystal clear and sparkling with purpose.

"It is time," Varik said "to choose sides. Each Court must decide: will they fight for the living to unite the realm? Or will they ally with Ereda and her undead horde ? The Lords and Ladies are gathered here. There will not be a feast. There will instead be a Reckoning."

He reached for Arianette. When their fingers met, that strange energy that was always simmering between them surged, stronger than ever. Arianette drew in close to him. Asheron watched as they walked out of the room together, Lorna trailing behind.

"A moment, if you please, Enchantress," he called out.

Lorna turned back around to face Asheron as Varik and Arianette fled the room hand in hand.

162

CHAPTER 26

THE UNBINDING

Varik did not bring Arianette back to her chambers. Instead, he escorted her to his own. They were no less grand than his chambers at the Sky Court. Though Asheron's words may have trod a line that bordered on disrespect, he had not slighted the Skylord in this. There was evidence, also, of Lorna's failed diversion. Platters of rich foods were strewn about, along with decanters of nectar and Faery wine. The whole tableau brought back that first evening in Varik's quarters to Arianette.

"Wine?" Varik asked. He no longer looked so composed and full of purpose. His wings fluttered wildly and sweat beaded on his brow.

Arianette nodded, mute, disconsolate. Varik poured two glasses but only half full. He handed one to Arianette, who sipped it. The other he held, not drinking it, just swirling it idly.

"I want you to know," he began, "that I did not make the geis with you because of the prophecy and power it might bring to me." Arianette looked as if she was about to protest, but Varik raised a hand, silencing her.

"Can you not feel the bond between us, Arianette? We were *made* for one another. We are each other's destiny," Varik said.

There was something like fear in his eyes when he looked up to meet her eyes. The force, the draw, the intense longing that was a magic of its own pulsed between them again. Varik moved closer to Arianette, slow and controlled, as she stood motionless, watching the feline grace of his approach.

"May I," he asked, cautious, "see it again?"

Arianette knew what he meant.

The rune.

With a questioning look, Varik placed his hand on her collarbone, eliciting that impassioned yearning that filled Arianette whenever he touched her. She nodded her assent as he peeled her robes aside, revealing the sharp edges of her shoulder blades, her rounded ivory breasts. Between them the rune pulsed.

Varik reached out to touch it.

"Don't," Arianette whispered, remembering what had happened to Lorna when she had touched the rune.

Varik drew one hand to her lips, running his index finger over them and silencing her protests. Then, ever so slowly, he moved his other hand so that his palm pressed against the rune.

Arianette sucked in her breath with a hiss as the Painbringer throbbed to the beat of her heart. The glass fell from her hand, crystal shattering against the gold tiled floor.

Varik ignored this, his expression grim, his lips turned down in a frown of concentration.

"What are you doing?" Arianette choked out, fear welling in her belly. Varik didn't answer with words. He answered with a surge of magic that made her bones ache as his power flowed into her. Her heartbeat raced and her skin crawled with static as if she were a vessel on the receiving end of a lightning strike.

She gasped.

Varik looked up and met her eyes, his gaze calm, determined.

"Do you trust me, Arianette?" he whispered, hand still pressed against her chest, power still flowing between them, pumping into her. Did she? She desperately wanted to trust Varik.

"Yes," she breathed, closing her eyes and letting herself sink into his embrace.

He pressed harder against the rune. A shudder wracked Arianette's body. Then Varik pulled her even closer, and pressed his lips against her.

Arianette felt as if she were slipping her own skin, as if she were somehow being torn from her own body. Half formed memories that could not be her own poured into her mind in a relentless torrent.

For what felt like a long time she could only stand there with her eyes squeezed closed as her body changed around her, muscles shifting and morphing. A burning tension shot straight up her spine.

Then she felt them. Her wings. They burned like a thousand shards of broken glass slamming into her vertebrae as they burst free, unfurling behind her.

Her eyes flew open.

It was like seeing the world for the first time. Every color brighter, every sound more intense, a sickening, swirling kaleidoscope that bowled her over, made her choke. Her mind swam, unable to make sense of her surroundings, of all the scenes playing in rapid staccato images through her head. She could not focus on anything, it was all a cacophony. Pure. Chaos.

"Varik," she moaned. Dimly, she recognized that he was on his knees before her, gazing reverently up at her.

"Arianette," Varik whispered. "I've unbound you."

He placed a hand on her cheek.

And Arianette screamed.

CHAPTER 27

THE FALLING SKY

The guards streamed into the chambers, ready to battle whatever terror lay before them, but they found only Varik on his knees over the prostrate form of Arianette, running his fingers through her scarlet hair, trying to soothe her hysterics.

"Get the Shadow sorceress, Lorna Blackburn. Quickly now," Varik ordered. There was panic in his eyes and his face was so pale it was almost the sickly gray of an Accursed.

The guards rushed off. It did not take long for them to return with Lorna. She drew her hand to her mouth, horrified as she gazed upon the scene before her. Arianette, collapsed on the ground, shrieking, pure white wings like those of an angel protruding through the shredded fabric of her robe. Varik, kneeled above her, shaking and murmuring.

"What have you done?" Lorna demanded.

"I only meant to-" Varik gestured futilely at Arianette.

Lorna rushed over kneeling with Varik beside her.

"I know what you meant to do," Lorna snapped. "You meant to unbind her. You used your magic and the rune to do it after Asheron told you that this might happen."

It did not seem possible for Varik to grow more ghostly, yet somehow he did when he met Lorna's furious glare.

"I didn't think—"

"That's your problem Varik, you never think. You're like a child. First you banish Braedin when we are surrounded by enemies and need every ally we can get. And why? Because you were *jealous*. Jealous that he loved her. Then, you do this to the very girl you're supposed to be protecting ," Lorna , who almost never spoke in anger , shouted, disgusted.

Arianette's screams died down to sobs. Lorna took her face in her hands.

"Arianette, it is me, Lorna. Tell me what is wrong," she crooned, stroking her tousled hair. Arianette looked up, green eyes bright and glassy, but she did not answer. Her eyes rolled back in her head. Only the whites showed as she was lost to her own memories.

5

The sky was falling on a city made of crystal, shattering around her. Fire lit the air, ice shards pelted down, and the streets ran red as blood mingled with sea water. Someone held her hand; her mother, Amabella. Amabella's hair was teal green instead of flaxen, her ears slender and pointed.

This was not Amabella, the Wood Witch of the Green Wood, this was Amabella the Elven slave. It must be so for her around her wrists were tattooed chains, and beneath each eye they had tattooed the tiny flames that marked her as property of the Fire Court.

Around them, through the cacophony of breaking glass, a voice was indistinct yet penetrating near Arianette's ear.

"Go. Go with your mother to the Heart of the Forest. Hurry. The hour draws near when we must seal the Veil. The Glass City is lost."

The man was tall and slender as a wisp with flaming red hair and black eyes pin pricked with tiny stars, a crystal circlet set upon his brow. His wings spread out behind him, white as snow.

"I will not leave you here to die alone, Somnium," the Elven Amabella sobbed, clutching the man with one hand and her daughter with the other. Tears streamed down her sharply protruding cheek bones.

"You do not leave me alone, Amabella. I remain here with so many others, with my people. This is as it should be. If we must perish, I must be by their side, but you— and she –" the man pressed a delicate hand to Arianette's brow, brushing her hair back from her pale forehead, "must carry on. She is our dream for the future. She may well be the last of your line and mine, when this is all done. She must live, Amabella. She must survive. She is our hope for the future, the prophecy we leave behind."

Amabella sobbed and threw her arms around the man who was Arianette's father. Her lips found his in a brief passionate kiss.

"I will bring her. It will be done" she choked out.

A tremendous crash overhead sent shattered fragments of stone and crystal hurtling towards them. Arianette screamed, but Somnium gestured and a shield of white light sprang up around them.

"Go now," he whispered, touching Arianette on the head. A warm glow crept over her skin. "Be not afraid child."

"Arianette come," Amabella said.

5

"Arianette, come back. Arianette, Arianette," someone repeated her name over and over. She felt a sudden rush, as if all of her blood was electrified, then the sensation of arms wrapped around her body. She could still hear someone whispering over and over in her ear.

"Arianette, come back. Come back to us Arianette."

Her eyes fluttered, irises turning from milky white to crystal green once again. She sucked in a deep ragged breath and looked around. Lorna was holding her as if she were a child, Varik was still on his knees before her, his hands gripping her arms so hard that they left bruises on the delicate flesh. He looked wild eyed and desperate. Behind him Arianette saw red and gold traced tapestries hanging on the wall. The Court of Flames. She was back in the Court of Flames.

"I – was – there. I saw my mother. And my father," she stammered.

"Where? Arianette, are you all right?" Varik shook her so hard in his desperation that her teeth knocked together.

"Varik, let her go," Lorna ordered.

The Skylord released his grip, looking abashed, but did not break eye contact with Arianette.

"What did you see, Arianette?" he asked.

"The Court of Dreams, the day they closed the Veil. I was there. I remember."

"That's not possible. You're –" Varik almost said just a girl. But she wasn't, was she? She had never been just a girl. He stared at her wings; downy, white feathered, shimmering things. What creature did they come from?

"Arianette, your father. Who was your father?" There was something avid in his eyes, something hungry that Arianette flinched away from.

"Varik, be quiet." Lorna stroked Arianette's hair gently. But Arianette looked up and met Varik's gaze steadily. There was something he'd never seen before in her expression. It was almost like an unfamiliar person was staring back at him.

"Somnium," she said, setting her chin. "My father was Somnium, Lord of the Dreamers." Lorna and Varik both froze, as if struck.

"How do you know?" Varik asked, his voice very low as he struggled to maintain his composure.

"I told you, I remember. There is much that I remember now," Arianette said, cryptic. She closed her eyes, trying to block out another wave of memory threatening to pass over her.

Lorna and Varik exchanged concerned looks. Somnium had been dead many long years. Arianette was right, though, at the time of the Culling, he had been the unquestionable Lord of the Dream Fae.

Which meant that Arianette was, at the very least, a true Queen. She was the last of the Dreamer bloodline. Hence, the rightful heir to the Court of Dreams. If she reclaimed her throne, the Elven blood on her mother's side would be called into question. But as the *last* Dreamer. It was more likely than not she could claim the crown, if she wanted to reign over the wreckage of the Broken Lands.

"Varik. We need to get her out of here. The last Dreamer? If Asheron finds out and tells Ereda... a living heir to the Dreamer's throne? My sister would not let her live." Lorna's voice rang with alarm.

For a moment Varik continued kneeling before Arianette, gazing at her as if entranced. Then he steepled his fingers and shook his head.

"No," he said softly. "We stay. Arianette, would you claim your birthright tomorrow, at the Reckoning?"

Her green eyes flashed; flashed with something he had never seen in them before.

They flashed with purpose.

"Varik, surely you cannot mean to-"

"I will claim what is mine," Arianette announced, interrupting Lorna's protest.

Varik smiled at her then, a cool calculating thing, and Arianette matched it.

"And the geis?" Still smiling he arched an eyebrow at this new, changed Arianette sitting before him.

"I will honor my geis. I will unite the Court of Sky and the Court of Dreams," Arianette said coolly.

Lorna glanced from Varik, who looked rather like the cat who'd just gotten away with eating the canary, to Arianette and shook her head.

"Perhaps I should leave you two to make your plans for domination of the Realms," Lorna said, rolling her eyes.

Arianette blinked up at Lorna.

"Perhaps you should," she agreed without a touch of warmth in her voice. Lorna looked hurt by this cursory dismissal, but Varik waved her off.

"Leave us for a spell, Lorna," Varik said. She did not want to go, did not like the way they were studying one another. But she could not protest. Lorna bowed deeply. Perhaps a bit too deeply to be sincere, and strode from the room without a sound.

When she had gone, Varik took Arianette's hands and pulled her to her feet. He grazed his hands over her wings, lightly tracing the lines of them. They twitched beneath his touch. Then he ran his fingertips over her narrow dagger-like ears.

"You are stunning," Varik said. Arianette jerked away from him, folding her wings behind her back.

"You had no right to do this to me," she accused, her voice steel, her eyes harder.

Varik flinched at the unexpected accusation.

"Arianette, I am sorry," he floundered.

Arianette let out a bitter burst of laughter.

"No, you're not. You've just gotten what you wanted all along. It's just as Lorna said. The Skylord always gets what he wants." Varik frowned, brow furrowing in frustration.

"Arianette from the very first moment I met you, I felt this power deep within you. But I also felt something else. I felt that power between *us*. I felt our bond."

Arianette smirked.

"It seems you're rather good at breaking bonds," she said, her face stony.

"Don't say that, Arianette. Please don't say that. The bond between you and me –"

"If there was such a bond, then why the geis in the first place? Why force my hand?" she asked bitterly.

Varik looked up then, his sky blue eyes glittering .

173

"Because I was afraid I would lose you then. Just as I'm afraid I will lose you now. *You* are my destiny. I don't care a whit about the prophecy. Whether you're the daughter of a Wood Witch, or the Legion Queen. You are the only thing I want, the only thing I have wanted in so long. I love you, Arianette. Say you love me too."

She looked up at him and her eyes were green as venom.

"I cannot say that. Not right now."

Varik stared after her as she walked out of his chambers, her white wings dragging behind her.

CHAPTER 28

THE BOUND AND THE BROKEN

M uírgan knew the moment they shattered the binding. Braedin was sitting beside her at the divining pool when suddenly his body bucked and he ground his teeth so hard she thought he might break them.

She did not need to ask what was wrong.

"Arianette," he gasped.

And with that name, she knew.

It was delicate work, an unbinding of that nature. The damnable Fae, in their impatience, had used a hammer when a file would have sufficed. For an immortal race they were always in such a hurry.

Muírgan sighed. She would have spared the girl the pain and confusion of shattering her Mortal veil like that, but what was done, was done. She wondered which of the fools had done it. Not Asheron, he could be hot tempered at times but was surprisingly level headed for a Fire Fae. He would not want a threat like a half-Elven Dreamer raised as a Mortal running amok in the Realms. A Legion Queen was a threat to his reign. To all the Fae Court's reigns. And while the dark sorceress might have wished to test her skills,

Muírgan did not think she was powerful enough to break the binding by herself, nor foolish enough to try.

The Skylord then. That vain fool Varik Skyborn must have done it.

"Something has happened to Arianette." Braedin's voice jarred Muírgan from her thoughts. He stared at her with wide haunted eyes.

Muírgan nodded somberly at him.

"The last Dreamer has awakened."

Braedin looked confused.

Muírgan backpedaled, seeing that he did not understand. Goddess the Fae were so thick.

"Arianette is the daughter of Somnium and Lady Amabella Gracelilly, who was once an Elven Princess, later an Elven slave. Bound in a Mortal body as she was, Arianette could not have known this. But now, with our help," *and the meddling of your fool brother,* she thought. "We have re-awakened her true self. She is the Legion Queen. She represents all of the races. If the prophecy is true, she will one day rule the Realms."

Braedin's eyes slowly widened as the implications of this became apparent to him.

"Do you wish to help her, Braedin Redwing? If you do, I can teach you. We can build the bond. We can win her to our side." There was a gleam in Muírgan's eye.

Braedin furrowed his brow. Something about this sounded wrong, manipulative. But the very idea of Arianette here, beside him, *bound* to him... he smelled juniper on the wind.

"What do I need to do?"

"Come with me, Braedin Redwing."

Muírgan led Braedin to the Drowning Pool. The waters were still as glass, mirroring their reflections as they stood side by side. Braedin was golden, with his proud fierce antlers and his powerful wings. Muírgan was tall and willowy with sharply curved ears, and wide set feline eyes.

"Do you trust me, Braedin Redwing?" Muírgan asked. She dipped a finger into the pool. Ripples spread out from the point of contact, contorting their images.

"More than I trust some, less than I trust others," Braedin said, gruff.

Muírgan laughed at that.

"You are wise beyond your years, Braedin. The power of water is the power of change. A river can create a valley where once there was only stone. The sea can change the face of a shoreline. And see how one tiny stone," Muírgan took a small pebble and tossed it in the pool. "Can send out ripples that have the power to change everything? That will be us. We will be the ripple in the water that becomes a tidal wave." She gave him a measured look.

"How will this help Arianette?"

"I would expose you to the elements so you might use them. But you must trust me each step of the way. To study water is to study change. And I fear you might find Arianette changed, when next you meet."

Braedin studied Muírgan. Her eyes were the color of spring grass and in them he could see the weight of a thousand lifetimes. The Elves were a far older race than the Fae. They had ruled the Ethereal Realms for Millennia before being conquered. And if Muírgan had her way, they might rule again. She was proud, she was powerful, and she had a seductive vision for the future of the realm.

"I trust you enough," Braedin annunciated each word.

"Good," she said. "Then let us begin." She moved around behind him, her thin supple body pressing up against his.

"You must give to the Great Mother Xennia, the Lady of this lake, your breath. In return she will give you her power." Muírgan locked eyes with Braedin. There was no hesitation in his golden gaze.

He was prepared.

Muírgan placed her spindly fingers to the base of his skull, applying pressure and pushing his head down towards the rippling surface of the pool.

His body offered resistance for a moment as his face grazed, then slipped beneath, the surface of the water. But that happened with all of them. Fae, Elf, and Mortal alike balked at that first touch of icy water upon their lips. Every soul perceived the threat. No man was willing to perish without a fight.

Muírgan pushed harder.

Braedin ceased resisting as his head dipped beneath the surface. His golden hair fanned out in the water. For a few minutes bubbles streamed up from beneath the surface.

Then the bubbles ceased.

Braedin's body bucked beneath her hands, but Muírgan's slight stature was deceptive. Within her willowy frame lay the supernatural strength and prowess of the Elven kind.

She kept him submerged until he ceased all motion and hung limp over the edge of the pool. She was not as spry as

178

she had once been. It took all her strength to haul Braedin's lifeless bulk from the pool, but she managed it.

Muírgan worked quickly, arranging his form in the reeds, tracing the pattern of runes on his brow with her ink, then speaking the invocation that would restore him.

"Eta eritana luxiana," she pressed her mouth against Braedin's and whispered the words into it.

His eyes flew open; still golden but flecked, now, with tiny specks of deep blue.

"It is done," Muírgan said, gazing into those eyes.

For a moment he spluttered, coughing and spitting up the pool water. Then a slow smile spread across Braedin's face. He glanced at the still waters of the pool and curled a single finger. A thin rivulet of water sprang from the pool, obeying his command. It split into myriad droplets, forming a halo around Muírgan's head, then froze there, a perfect crown of ice wreathing her hair. He released the spell and they fell to the ground with a quiet tinkling. Then they melted and were gone.

"You learn fast, Braedin Redwing," Muírgan said with approval. "But even so, there is much that you do not know."

CHAPTER 29

THE RECKONING

They held the Reckoning outside in an amphitheater where the Fire Fae traditionally held gladiator battles between the slaves. Elven and Fae blood still smeared the gold flooring.

Varik was the first to enter through the golden arches, being the Lord who had called the Reckoning into effect. Lorna flanked him on his left, regal in her black robes slashed with the blue and silver that marked her as a member of the Sky Court.

On his right side, where Braedin had once always stood tall and proud, was Arianette. She wore a backless white chiffon gown with lace capped sleeves and a long train. Her wings, the pristine white of a snowy dove's, extended out from her shoulder blades for all the Fae Lords and Ladies to see.

She took a seat beside Varik at the head of a massive table, gazing out, her green eyes affecting no emotion.

Asheron was the next to enter. He looked resplendent in armor that glinted like a living burning thing as it caught the light of the setting sun. He flickered with red and gold flames, surrounded by his Flame Bearers, the most powerful wizards of his Court.

After Asheron came Lady Nimione, the ruler of the Sea Court, wearing a sleek turquoise gown, slit high up both sides to reveal shimmering scales running the length of her legs. She walked with tiny elegant steps, for as lovely as her scaled legs were, they were weak. The Merfolk relied upon their powerful tailfins in their own Court. Nimione's daughters surrounded her. The seven siren were all similarly clad and tiptoed daintily to their places.

It seemed Nimione had not deemed it necessary to bring Titus, her common blooded King Consort, with her.

"Where is your second, Varik Skyborn? Your lieutenant? You've traded your golden warrior for this mongrel harlot?" Nimione tittered. Her voice was high and sweet, but her tone was cutting. It was said the mermaids of the Sea Court used their lovely voices to lure lesser Fae to watery graves for sport.

Cruel Nimione, it seemed, would prove to be a difficult ally for Varik to win over.

Last came the delegation from the Court of Earth. Two Fae men with insectile wings, huge, covered from head to toe in metal armor, massive war axes strapped to their backs. Anduin and Alarkin said nothing, making their way to their seats at the table with purpose and sitting erect in their spots. They looked around with hooded eyes at the assembly.

Two empty seats remained.

The ruined Dream Court could expect no delegate. The Shadow Court's ruler, the Empress Ereda, Lorna's shadowy sister, had not been invited.

But Ereda had never been one to wait for an invitation. As the Fae Lords looked around, appraising one another,

181

Ereda appeared like an exhalation of smoke rising from a thick gray mist in the hall. She wore black leather and lace studded with silver barbs. A long snakelike whip rested at her hip.

"You break the sacred Fae tradition of Entete Cordial, Varik Skyborn, by not inviting me," Ereda crooned. A pulse of alarm that was almost tactile spread throughout the delegates at the table.

"I do not recognize the legitimacy of your Court, Lady Ereda Blackburn . The council is within their rights in denying you a voice at this Reckoning," Varik said, stiffening.

"Wrong, Lord Varik. Would that you were even half the man your father was. But, for all his wisdom, he is dead. Along with the rest of your line . Yet, still you seek to insult me. You're a fool, Varik Skyborn." Ereda ticked her tongue and floated into the center of the circle.

Hands fell to rest upon sword belts. Defensive spells hovered on the tips of tongues, but Ereda raised her hands in a placating gesture.

"Despite the Skylord's claims, I do not seek to wage war on my fellow Fae. You all believe that my armies linger on the Sky Court borders to threaten Lord Skyborn. They do not." Ereda looked around the table, scowling. "I have gathered my Accursed to face a threat far greater than a Skyborn could ever pose. They are there to face the threat in the South."

Varik bristled at the insult but maintained his composure.

"You deny that you pose a threat to Varik and the Sky Court?" Asheron asked, arching an eyebrow.

The other Lords and Ladies whispered amongst themselves, unsure what to make of this turn of events. Arianette sat with eyes narrowed, blazing with hatred as she watched Ereda Blackburn.

"Oh I wouldn't *mind* claiming his little Court as a spoil of war. But I wouldn't need an army of –"

"Accursed. You poison our people with your stolen spells. Your army is an aberration." Varik pounded his fist upon the table.

The Shadow Empress did not even flinch.

"Call them what you will. I do not need the Accursed to take the Sky Court. I could do it with my Shadow Weavers alone. Just ask my sister, she'll tell you." Ereda cut a black look at Lorna, who sat beside Varik looking pale and drawn.

"The army of the Sky Court is untried and untrained. Varik, you have never had an eye for war craft like your father did. Your half-brother might have been able to figure out some way to best me. But now he, too, is gone. Just like the rest of your family, and your allies of old, the Dreamers. Your list of friends is short, Lord Skyborn."

Varik clenched his fists so tightly that his knuckles turned white. Air churned wildly around him. Lorna placed a hand on his arm.

"She is trying to get under your skin," she hissed in Varik's ear.

"Well, it's working," Varik growled through clenched teeth.

Then Arianette stood. Her flame red hair, Dreamer hair, streamed in Varik's windstorm as she spread her an -gelic wings.

"The Dreamers," she declared, "are not all gone."

She beat her wings and took to the sky. All eyes were on her as she soared over Ereda's head. When she landed, it was in the seat reserved for the delegate from the Court of Dreams.

"Varik's mongrel tart? Who is this girl and what is the meaning of this?" Nimione's voice broke the stunned silence. Varik turned to Nimione.

"She is the daughter of the Dream lord Somnium—"

"She is the bastard daughter of one of Asheron's Elven slaves." Ereda scoffed and waved a dismissive hand in Arianette's direction.

Arianette did not acknowledge the insult. She stood rigid, her hands balled into fists at her sides.

"My mother was Amabella Gracelilly, an Elven Princess. My father was Somnium, Lord of the Court of Dreams. I am their legacy. As the last Dreamer, I claim their throne."

Hushed murmurs rippled through the room, but it was Ereda who finally answered her claim.

"Claim your throne, mongrel. It makes no difference to me," Ereda said with a sneer. "I will destroy you, and the Skylord, and my turncoat sister. But your 'Kingdom' is the threat here. You may claim to rule the Court of Dreams, but there is another Queen in the Broken Lands and she is the only Queen who worries me."

"What Queen do you speak of Ereda? What threat? Enough riddles," Asheron growled.

"You yourself admitted the Dreamers have been gone for centuries now, and they were never much of a threat in the first place, except on a philosophical level. You saw to their destruction yourself during the Culling. Which was done under *your* command," Nimione twittered, looking bored,

Ereda narrowed her eyes at the mermaid Lady.

"How quickly we forget that a Reckoning took place, very much like this, and every Fae Liege Lord down to a man signed his name in blood to the decree. Except The Skylord and the Lord of the Dreamers. Yet somehow now the whole lot of it was at my command? I do not want war amongst the Courts, but *she*," Ereda pointed a narrow finger at Arianette, "is a threat to us all."

The weighty black pressure of Ereda's gaze fell heavily upon Arianette. She raised her head and set her chin defiantly. Across the table, Varik leapt to his feet slamming his palms down on the table.

"How dare you—"

"Oh, I am quite daring—"

"Do not even look at her, witch," Varik warned. The wind had kicked up around him and was swirling, but with some effort he forced his fury and magic to stay contained.

Nimione drummed her fingernails on the table, looking bored, while Anduin and Alakar whispered to each other, deep frowns cut into their stony faces.

"That's enough of this" Nimione said. "I've no interest in where the Skylord sows his seed. And if the girl wants to rule over a barren wasteland let her have at it. I am more interested in this other threat. I know we come from beneath the waves and aren't always up on current events, but I've heard of no threat to the south since the Elves raised the Court of Dreams.

Across the table one of the Earth Fae cleared his throat. He wore a irritated expression on his face.

"Aye, what of this threat?" Alarkin rumbled.

Ereda whipped around to face them.

"Fools, do you not hear the whispers amongst the lesser Faeries? Surely even beneath the mountains and under the waves the smallfolk speak of strange stirrings in the Broken Lands."

Nimione responded with a tsk of her tongue and a flick of her webbed fingers.

"The lesser Fae always have their whispered gossip and tall tales," she said in her sibilant voice.

"The Elves amass an army even now," Ereda snapped.

"Enough of this foolishness." Varik raised his hand to silence the murmuring in the room.

Silence descended like a shroud.

"We decide today," he declared. "Choose your sides. Ereda claims she is not the enemy. But we have all seen her army of undead. My people, my kinsmen, walk amongst her Accursed, never to experience the peace of the Void. Yours do, as well. Will you stand with me against her? Will you stand with the Court of Sky and the Court of dreams? Or will you side with evil again."

Varik made eye contact with Arianette across the hall. She nodded, almost imperceptible. She might be angry with him over the unbinding, furious even. But she was on his side in this.

It seemed she was the only one.

Nimione fidgeted in her seat, avoiding Varik's steady gaze. Anduin and Alarkin frowned, arms folded across their chests, stoic and silent.

It was Asheron who broke the silence.

"Then Asheron, looking wistful, finally broke the silence.

"Both Ereda and Varik have offered nothing but friendship to the people of the Court of Flames. I will not have bad blood between us. I'm sorry, Lord Skyborn, the Court of Fire remains neutral." He sounded apologetic, but firm.

He would not be swayed.

Alarkin, the larger of the two tower giants from the Court of Earth cleared his throat.

"We who dwell beneath the Realms have problems of our own to deal with. The Gremlins and Blue Caps run amok. We cannot spare the resources for another point-less battle between rival Courts," he growled, pursing his lips.

Varik's face fell, his fists uncurled and the churning air around him stilled when Nimione chimed in.

"The Court of Sea chooses neither side. We have trou-bles enough beneath the waves. And if what Ereda says is true, we must prepare ourselves to wage war on this mighty band of Elves," Nimione tittered.

The silence in the room spoke volumes. Varik's jaw ticked as he ground his teeth and crumpled back into his seat.

"None will stand with you Lord Skyborn. But I have heard your call to arms. Your Court and mine. To the win-ner goes the spoils."

Ereda removed a black glove and flung it on the table.

A declaration of war.

Varik flinched back from it and when he looked up again, there was fear in his eyes.

"Give me your Dreamer, Varik, and spare your people a war they cannot possibly win. Otherwise, prepare to go the way of the Dreamers and the Elves, Skyborn."

Ereda did not look triumphant as she spoke. The Shadow Empress only looked pensive. She was not even looking at Varik as she spoke. She was gazing up at the twilit sky. And the falcon circling there.

Varik got back to his feet, chair screaming against stone as he pushed it back from the table. Wind swirled through the room, magic just barely contained.

"You will all be sorry," he snarled, baring his teeth.

He stretched his crystalline wings and flew to Arianette's side. He took her hand and raised their twined fingers skyward.

"By the power of the Goddess, here, before the eyes of the Lords and Ladies of all the Fae Courts, I soul-fast myself to Arianette Gracelilly, last of the Dreamers, daughter of the union between the Wood Witch Amabella, who was an Elven Princess, and Somnium, the Lord of the Dreamers." Varik paused, turning his eyes to Arianette, the filament of desire reverberated between them.

"The Courts of Sky and Dreams unite in opposition to the Shadow Empress," Arianette intoned.

The air swirled around them, glowing brightly, engulfing them in a storm of bright light.

Lorna, Nimione, Alarkin and Anuin, even Asheron stared at them, jaws slack, eyes wide with amazement.

Only Ereda did not share in the wonder.

She spat on the floor at their feet.

"You and your mongrel stand alone then, Skylord. Against all the might of the Shadow Court," she declared.

Then she drew her cloak of shadows around herself and was gone.

As the wind and light came under control again, Arianette cast her eyes around the room.

"You will all be sorry for the decisions you made here today," she said.

Then, hand still locked in Varik's, they strode from the hall with their heads held high. Lorna trailed behind them looking pale, drawn, and afraid.

They made their way in silence down the cobbled path that led from the amphitheater back to the Flame Palace. The mood shifted as the gravity of all that had happened sank in.

"A word, Arianette, if you would," Lorna said as they approached the door to her chambers. She nodded to Lorna and extricated her hand from Varik's grip.

"Go to your quarters," Arianette said to Varik. "Do not wait for me."

And although he had seen her present herself as a Queen at the Reckoning and should not have been surprised by the note of command in her voice... he was.

For a moment Varik hesitated. Then he dipped his head in consent.

"Come inside," Arianette said to Lorna indicating the door with a tilt of her head.

CHAPTER 30

NEW MARKINGS

"You have new runes," Lorna said, once they were alone. She was careful to keep her voice casual. Arianette's fingers drifted to her forehead where the most obvious of the new markings had appeared. Undáe, the rune for ripple, wave, change.

"I have several. And new memories to go with them."

"And powers?" Lorna arched a black brow.

Arianette narrowed her eyes at the sorceress. She raised her hand and whispered a word. A black orchid appeared in her palm. She motioned with her other hand and a small orb of white light appeared around the orchid for an instant. Then the flower exploded into a shower of white sparks.

Lorna watched, mesmerized. These were spells that had not existed in the Realms since the Culling. Elven magic. Dream weaving. She cleared her throat, looking slightly uncomfortable.

"I see. That is impressive. But how are you feeling? This must be a lot to make sense of."

Arianette cut a sharp look at Lorna.

"What do you mean?" she snapped.

190

Lorna raised her hands, deflecting the anger she sensed in Arianette's rigid posture.

"I only meant a lot has happened, and so quickly. It was not so long ago that you were only the daughter of a Wood Witch. Thrust into another life, bearing the burden of two different pasts. It can't be easy. So I ask, how are you, Arianette?"

Arianette balled her hands into fists and looked away.

"It doesn't matter how I am. Who I am is all that has every mattered to any of you. What I am is what matters. That is why you dragged me across the wretched Veil in the first place, is it not? Because you thought I was the Legion Queen." Blood dripped from her palms where he nails bit into the flesh. "So I will be your Legion Queen. I will burn anyone who stands in my way to the ground to reclaim my birthright. What more do you want of me?"

Lorna studied Arianette for a moment, the rigidity of her stance, the way her ivory wings twitched at the base of her spine, the grimace plastered across her face.

"Be careful, Arianette, when you gaze into the Void, as you do now. The reflection that stares back is a seductive thing. I know you see power. I know you see revenge. Do not let it lure you in too deep. Do not forget your humanity in all of this. It is the one thing the rest of us lack. The one thing you have that no other Queen can claim in these lands. It is what makes you Legion. A Queen for all the Realms and all the races."

Arianette tossed her head back and laughed bitterly.

"Do not speak to me," she said, "of the Void as if you know what it is to gaze into it, Lorna Blackburn. You might know the shadows, but you have not seen the abyss."

191

Lorna bowed her head.

"And Varik?" she asked.

"What of the Skylord?"

"Will you honor your geis? You are soul-fasted to him."

"Yes. I remain geis-bound to Varik Skyborn. And now I'm soul-fasted to him. I will honor our agreement. I will stand beside him and fight, when the time comes," Arianette said.

She seemed distracted now, engrossed in braiding her hair into one of the elaborate chignons favored by the Elves. The pointed tips of her ears peeked out from beneath the braids and curls.

Lorna could tell that nothing would come of pressing her further on this topic. She sighed and smiled wanly at Arianette.

"Well, that is good to hear. We will need a united front if we hope to defeat my sister in the days to come."

Arianette's head snapped up and her eyes alighted on Lorna, full of anguish and rage.

"Your sister will die by my hand for the things she has done. She killed my family. She destroyed my legacy. I will end her. Mark my words," Arianette vowed.

Lorna shivered and cleared her throat.

"That is what she deserves. Just do not underestimate Ereda, she is—"

"Ereda is nothing," Arianette growled, securing her locks with a tourmaline hairpin.

Lorna squirmed, uncomfortable.

"Yes, well. I'll leave you to prepare. We leave at dusk, for the Sky Court under cover of darkness."

Arianette nodded absently, pinning a final stray curl high up on her head.

5

Lorna was shaken. She needed to speak to Varik. She had grown fond of Arianette over the days and weeks since she'd brought her across the Veil. She thought of her as a friend; a little sister even.

But the girl Lorna had just spoken to was not the Arianette she knew. Was the coldness, the hardness, just an act to hide the turmoil inside? A mask to cover the confusion of two unique histories, two disconnected lives, trapped within one mind?

Or was the Wood Witch's daughter gone, replaced by this avenging angel of a girl?

Varik's door was slightly ajar, so Lorna toed it open and ducked into his chambers. Torches danced in a breeze that could only be Varik's uncontained magic, as the windows were closed. They had cleared away the feast but there were still several wine decanters laid out. Two sat upright, a third was overturned, leaking crimson liquid onto the gold brocade table cloth.

Varik stood at a window, gazing out it as if he were staring straight into the Void. His silver hair was disheveled and he held a chalice in one hand.

"Varik?"

He turned and they locked gazes across the room. It was clear from his bloodshot eyes and flushed cheeks that he had been hitting those bottles hard already. Lorna wasn't surprised. This had always been Varik's way when the pressure weighed on him.

"May I come in?" she asked

The Skylord nodded, not looking at her. Lorna entered the chamber, closing the door behind her with a quiet click. She approached the window where Varik stood and placed a hand on his shoulder..

"Have I doomed my people to death at your sister's hands? What will we find when we return to the Sky Tower tomorrow?" Varik sounded lost, forlorn. He gazed out over the lands that separated him from his kingdom.

"It will take Ereda time to muster her army and march. We will come up with a plan."

She didn't mention that it was likely her sister would reap some kind of revenge on the Sky Court on her way back to the Court of Shadows.

Varik already knew this.

"I wanted to talk to you about Arianette," Lorna said carefully. Varik's eyes grew stormy and the magic in the room intensified. Lorna's gold and jet hair whipped back away from her face as the breeze kicked up. He didn't say a word, though, only watched her, waiting. Lorna suddenly felt that old discomfort again; that feeling that the weight of their history was pressing down on her.

She stepped away from the window and poured herself a glass of wine, hoping to steady herself before saying a piece that Varik would likely find unpalatable. She took a long sip, then began.

"I know Arianette says she will honor the geis, but I don't know that your soul-fasting was a good idea."

She expected Varik to rage, but instead he turned to her, his lip quirking up in a half smile.

"Don't tell me you're jealous, Blackburn. I thought those days were over."

Varik's eyes moved casually over Lorna as if he could see straight through her robes to the body that had once fit with his like a glove. Her narrow hips, her small firm breasts; she felt him trace them with his glassy blue eyes. She blushed and shook her head.

"No, Varik, it's not that."

"What then?"

"Haven't you seen the change in her since you unbound her? She's different. I don't trust her. I'm afraid she's – well, I'm afraid she might be dangerous."

Varik was sipping his wine as Lorna spoke, and when she uttered the word 'dangerous' he laughed so hard he nearly spat it across the room.

"Of course she's dangerous. Isn't that what we wanted? A warrior Queen to unite the Realms?"

Varik seemed to sober somewhat for a moment.

"Lorna, I am bound to her, not just by the geis, but by something else, something bigger."

"Do you love her?" the Shadow Sorceress asked softly.

Varik released a weighty sigh.

"More than anyone I have ever known," he replied.

Lorna thought she was past feeling jealousy over Varik Skyborn. But the words stung.

"Just know that she is not the same girl she once was," Lorna cautioned.

Varik stepped away from the window. He picked up one of the decanters and filled his glass.

"Lorna, none of us are who we once were," he said with a lopsided smile that brought a pang of longing to her heart, so intense that she could only turn and bolt from his chambers.

CHAPTER 31

FLEE

They fled the Court of Fire like thieves in the night. There was no caravan, no fanfare, only a single carriage, small but serviceable, with nothing to give it away as a vessel of the royal Court.

The mood in the carriage was as black as the cover of darkness they hid behind. Varik brooded. Lorna fretted. Arianette gazed impassively out the window, refusing to stir from a near catatonic state. The tension was palpable as they flew over the forest, desperate to reach the Sky Tower and see what revenge Ereda had wrought on her way back to the Court of Shadows.

It was a grisly scene that awaited them as they drew up to the tower. Five severed mounted on the barbican, their mouths open in silent screams. Below, a herd of at least two dozen Accursed prowled, reaching for the disembodied heads with their desperate grasping claws.

"Goddess Xennia," Lorna whispered, covering her mouth with her hands.

"Your sister has been here. As we knew she would," Varik snarled.

He trembled with rage, winds whipping up, blowing back the hair upon the decapitated Fae to reveal their faces.

Ereda's point was hard to miss. She hadn't chosen a few stray solitary Fae to execute. The Skyborn line was thin and scattered, but Ereda had made a point of finding Fae of Varik's bloodline to Unmake. These were third cousins, half uncles, and the like. These were the men who had risen to fill the power void after most of the Skyborns had been exterminated.

Arianette looked on the bloody scene with an expression of impassive hardness.

"I'll get rid of them," she said. Lorna grabbed at her arm, but Arianette brushed her aside. She strode towards the Accursed.

The spell she cast was like the one she'd cast on the trail the day when Varik had rescued her; the day of their first kiss. Now, though, it was effortless.

Arianette closed her eyes, thought about the roots springing forth, and they obeyed; bursting out from beneath the granite cobbles. The stone shattered, impaling the undead with shards.

The roots gripped them, dragging them down to the earth, shattering their bones.

She raised her left hand and curled it into a fist. A glowing white mist rose up from the ground with soft hiss.

The air crackled and the Accursed howled in unearthly agony. Then there was a boom, like a thunder clap, and then they were gone. Only a fine gray mist hanging in the air remained of the Accursed as the roots and mist seeped back into the earth.

Arianette stretched her angelic wings and flew to the barbican, where she started wrenching the bloody heads from the iron spikes. With a whisper, she encircled each one in a mist of golden light. Then they too vanished with a sound like a sigh.

When all had been disposed of, Arianette flew through the Sky Gate without a backward glance, leaving Varik and Lorna gazing after her, mute with wonder.

"You're sure you want to be soul-fasted to *that?*" Lorna asked. Varik swallowed hard and did not answer.

CHAPTER 32

CONNECTION

The moons were lilac; swollen, bloated in the star fractured sky over the Broken Lands. They were nearly full. If Arianette had been just a Mortal girl, she would be heading home soon. Back to Onerth. Out of his life forever.

But she was not just a girl. Muírgan had told him the truth about her origins after she'd forged their rune bond. Tonight his runes pulsed, ached. He felt Arianette's pain and confusion, reverberating beneath his skin.

He rolled over, burying his head in his hands, praying for Xennia to grant him sleep. That was the only release from his suffering.

Muírgan had not told him the bond would be like this. If she had, he might not have done it. Eventually, Muírgan said, she would learn to control the bond as he did. But for now, his days were filled with all of Arianette's spikes of emotion and the maddening scent of vetiver.

He pressed tentatively at the bond, hesitant to force himself into her mind. It still felt like a violation, this artificial connection Muírgan had forged with her ink.

Then Braedin felt her push back. Confusion and alarm tore through the bond and he shuddered against it.

Shh, it is okay. I only want to help. Braedin focused on sending the words to her. The panic on the receiving end diminished.

Who are you? Arianette shot back through the bond.

A friend. I want to help you.

Help me do what?

Help you reclaim the Realms. Help you destroy your enemies. Help you become the Legion Queen.

There was silence on the other end. For a moment Braedin was afraid that he'd made a mistake. He'd pushed too hard and frightened her away. Just when he was about to give up, her reply came through the bond.

Tell me how.

Braedin sucked his teeth. Muírgan's plan was solid. But how would Arianette take it? He knew she was changed, could feel she was changed. But could not stop picturing her as the frail frightened creature, cowering on her hands and knees in the courtyard of the Sky Tower.

First you must end your geis with the Skylord. Without breaking it.

How?

There is only one way.

The silence was resounding. For a full minute there was only static in his mind. The sound of confusion, uncertainty, hesitation.

Tell me your plan, Arianette replied at last.

CHAPTER 33

CATATONIA

The palace slept.

Outside the moons shone full and bright, high in the sky at the witching hour, glowing blue as the untouched surface of a lake above the Sky Court.

Arianette wandered. Clad only in an ivory night shift her bare feet were silent on the icy ivory floor of the Sky Tower. She moved as if in a dream, her eyes rolled back in her head so that only the whites were visible. In her left hand she clutched a single candle, wax dripping down the silver holder. She did not flinch as it slithered onto her pale fingers. In her other hand she held a sky blue brocade ribbon.

She felt along the walls in the dark until she found the corridor. A secret passage. She could not say how she knew of it. It wasn't a memory. It was a quiet voice whispering to her, telling her where to go. A voice she knew.

She slipped in behind the tapestry and her breath came easier, her heart beat slowed. Here she was safe. Here she was unseen. The voice would guide her.

Follow the passage. Ten steps straight ahead.

What was she afraid of? The runes were a misery. The ruins were anguish. The runes were horror. They crawled all over her body as she slept, new glyphs etching themselves into her skin every night. Dreams were restless things, full of a half remembered life.

Often she dreamt of her mother. Not the Mortal Wood Witch, but the Elf. And then there was the willowy red haired man in a crystal circlet and violet robes. Her father. Somnium. Both dead now, but alive in her mind. And always that nagging question: who are you, Arianette? And what are you so afraid of?

Turn left. Go on another twenty paces.

She followed the disembodied voice radiating in her mind.

There will be a door.

Arianette ran her fingers along the rough stone wall. She felt the indentation and let her candle fall. The silver holder clattered against the floor. The flame guttered. In the darkness, she pressed her body against the door, feeling it give way and open up. She passed through it, into the darkened chamber

Steady now. You know this is the best thing. For all of us. End the War before it begins. Claim the Court for your own.

Arianette knew this was the truth.

She tiptoed across the chamber, approaching the massive bed, and climbed up onto it. Kneeling, she reached towards the slumbering figure. Holding the ribbon taut in both hands, she lowered it down towards his throat, where magic and breath were being drawn.

"Arianette, what are you doing?" Varik's familiar voice startled her.

He was not supposed to wake up. This was not part of the plan.

Varik's hands clamped down on her shoulders. She shuddered, convulsed. Her eyes flickered white and then went green again.

"Varik," she breathed, letting the ribbon drop from her hands, which were shaking now. He sat up in the bed.

"I'm sorry," she mumbled, struggling to break free from his grasp, to flee his chambers. Varik did not release her. He pulled her closer so she was almost in his lap and snatched the ribbon up with one hand, still gripping her with the other.

"I get the feeling you didn't plan on tying me to the bed and having a romp."

Varik arched an elegant eyebrow at her, indicating the ribbon with a cock of his head.

"I – I'm not sure," she lied, even as the voice in her head reminded her not to say too much.

"Okay," he took a deep breath, staring at her. "How did you even get in here?" Varik's tone was a cross between confusion and suspicion.

She pointed a shaky finger towards the wall panel that was slightly askew.

"Through there," she said.

Varik's eyebrows shot up.

"And how did you know about that?" This was a question Arianette could not answer.

"Arianette," he said. "Look at me."

She tried to keep her eyes averted, but Varik had turned up his magic and she lacked the fight inside to disobey his command. She looked up at him and a charge passed between them. Their bond, struggling to link them.

Arianette fought it.

She would not let passion dictate her actions here. She did not know what she might do if she released the vice grip that held her emotions in check.

"Varik, no. You don't understand. This isn't—" she tried to explain herself, but her resolve was slowly slipping. Down, deep beneath the surface of his beautiful eyes.

"Arianette," he repeated her name, his voice low and husky "I love you, Arianette."

In one fluid motion, Varik pinned her against the headboard. He held her with his hands against the cold marble. And she found herself caught inside his steady blue gaze. Furtive shadows danced in dim torchlight. Arianette wanted to crawl into them and vanish. Instead she said:

"Varik. We need to talk."

End him now, the voice whispered in her mind.

And suddenly Arianette recognized it, though she did not know how it was possible.

The voice was Braedin Redwing's. She tried to block it out, to push it out of her mind, but she got the feeling that it was still there. She studied Varik, knowing now that she could not kill him. The moment was lost. The two of them would have to figure out a way to banish whatever demons lay between them.

They would have to fight this war. Side by side. As she had promised they would that day in his throne room.

"Varik," Arianette said, "I am not the girl Lorna came upon in the forest. I am not that frightened daughter of a Wood Witch," Arianette said, and though she spoke softly, her voice made the crystal chandeliers tremble. She unfolded her wings, as if to prove the truth behind her words.

"I know, and I owe you an apology. I should not have unbound you the way I did, after Asheron's warnings. I could have hurt you."

"Could have hurt me?"

There was fury in Arianette's voice. Her hands twitched at her sides as she tried to keep her magic from exploding unchecked. The air rippled around her flashing with flickering white lights. Varik had to hold a hand out to ward off her magic as her control faltered. He slammed power back, their spells fighting for dominance as he knelt over her on the bed.

It was Arianette who won the battle, her white light strangling Varik's wind. He choked out a cry as both his spell and breath caught in his throat.

Arianette grimaced, reining the magic back in. Varik fell back onto his side, gasping.

Arianette's expression softened as she moved to kneel beside him. She leaned over him and pressed her lips to his ear.

"I need you to understand me. I know that you thought you were helping when you unbound me. But now there is another person inside me, a forgotten child with memories, feelings, and powers that I hardly recognize. Things cannot be as they were before. I will honor the geis. And I will fight beside you in the battle to come. But do not think you can claim my magic, or my kingdom, as your own. I will stand and fight, for my mother, my father, and my people who were slaughtered and enslaved. I fight for them."

She paused, expression stony.

"For them. Not for you Varik Skyborn. Can you live with that?"

Varik stared at Arianette as if she were an alien creature. Then the faintest vestige of a grin crept to his lips.

"Your kingdom? You admit it, then. You are the Legion Queen."

"I do not know if I am the one the prophecy speaks of. But I know that I am the last Dreamer."

"I can live with anything, as long as I'm with you," he said.

He reached up and traced his finger along Arianette's jaw. She closed her eyes. A sigh slipped from her lips as his hands caught in her hair and pulled her close to him.

Arianette raked her nails down his torso. She moved in for a kiss; bit his lower lip. Kissed him again.

The evening descended into swirling wind and white light as their bodies joined again.

CHAPTER 34

THE TIME DRAWS NIGH

Braedin and Muírgan gazed into the heart of the forest. Muírgan had sent Aciperre ahead, as ever, to be her eyes and ears. Through his eyes they watched the Shadow Empress' army flowing like a black wave through the mountain passes and towards the Valley of the Ancients.

"The time draws nigh. Have you told the girl of our plan?" Muírgan asked.

Braedin nodded, staring out across the desolate mountaintops. Snow fell atop the summits of the highest peaks, but in the valleys and passes only a cold constant rain.

"She did not tell the others?"

Braedin shrugged.

"She said that she would not."

Muírgan nodded, somber. Many things hinged on their victory in this battle. If Arianette played the role Braedin had asked of her, it could be the first step towards reclaiming the Ethereal Realms for the Elves. .

If she did not, it could end their bid for power before it had even begun. The same held true of Braedin. Muírgan was confident that he, at least, would stay true to his word.

Arianette, though, was the wildcard in her deck. She knew she would destroy Ereda, given the chance.

As for the rest...

"I am trusting you with my entire army, Braedin Redwing. Aciperre will be by your side, but it is up to you to ensure all goes as planned with Arianette."

Braedin grimaced. There was no love lost between himself and Muírgan's Elven General. Aciperre reminded Braedin of his brother, vain and rash. And Arianette, though he had penetrated her mind through the runes, he was still uncertain.

Did she trust him enough to do the thing he'd asked of her?

She'd failed in Varik's chamber. If she'd succeeded in that task, Braedin would be the Skylord now, and this war would have been stopped in its tracks. But she had not deposed his brother, as Muírgan had wanted.

Would she disappoint them both again?

"I will do my best, my Queen."

Braedin stepped away from the emerald stone in the heart of the ash tree. He let out a long low whistle. The scarlet winged hippogriff appeared by his side. He did not shapeshift, though he could have, the newest trick Muírgan had taught him.

Instead he mounted it.

"I give you Xennia's blessing, Braedin Redwing," Muírgan said. She traced the symbol of Xennia in the air. It shimmered, golden, then vanished.

Resplendent in his armor, antlers polished to a high shine, Braedin let out a call reminiscent of an eagle's cry.

The Wood Witch's Daughter

The Elven army melted out of the forest and arrayed themselves behind him. He laid his heels into his familiar and took off, the army following, heading for the Valley of the Ancients.

CHAPTER 35

THE BEST LAID PLANS

Varik, Lorna, and Arianette gathered in the war room, standing around the massive table. No one had gathered in this room since Varik's father had planned that ill-conceived siege on the Shadow Court during the Culling.

They would not make the same mistakes as Vargas Skyborn, that had already been decided. Varik would not risk an assault on the Shadow Caverns. They must wait for Ereda to come to them if they had any hope of victory.

The Sky Tower was perched so high in the mountains that its spires scraped the clouds. Chiseled into the granite of the range itself, the palace was, from the ground, impregnable. The small rock cut where Arianette had run afoul of the Accursed was the only route up the mountain by land.

If Ereda's army wanted to take the palace, they would have to do it from the air.

But Varik was the Skylord, he controlled the winds, and whatever unnatural powers Ereda might have stolen from the Elves, she could not defeat the Skylord's army in his own skies. The winds would throw her troops back, shatter them upon the rocky bluffs of the range.

This might seem like a splendid thing. But it meant Ereda must draw Varik and his army out, no matter what it took. So she would pillage and destroy and let loose her army of Accursed to rampage the Sky Court until she forced Varik to fight on her terms.

They could no more let that happen than they could attack the Shadow Caverns outright.

"Is there any hope that the other Courts will come to our aid?" Varik asked Lorna.

She frowned and shrugged.

"There is always hope, if only because it is the one thing no one has figured out how to kill yet... but I would not rely on the other Courts. They made their intentions clear at the Reckoning," Lorna said.

The three of them stared down at the raised relief map of the Sky Court.

"We must meet them in the field, then. At their borders. We cannot let them come marauding through the Sky Court," Varik said. He looked weary. His silver hair was disheveled, and bruise blue circles clung beneath his hollow eyes.

"Meeting them in open combat on an even playing field would be suicide. She would end us all," Lorna protested.

Arianette let her green eyes drift over the map.

"Perhaps we must find a not so level playing field then," she murmured, still intent on the map.

An image of the map flashed in her mind, overlaying the one before her eyes.

Braedin again, no doubt.

When this war was done, she would find a way to get him out of her head.

She took a finger and drew it along a raised ridge near the border with the Shadowlands.

"See here? If this map is correct, the forces of shadow must enter through this valley here," she traced her finger along an indentation in the topography. "Unless they wish to risk the winds on the peaks."

"They would never risk the mountains," Lorna said, watching the motion of Arianette's finger along the map.

"Then they must pass through –"

"The Valley of the Ancients," there was a tinge of excitement in Varik's tone.

"We can hide in the passes. Ambush them as they come through the valley. They will never expect me to leave my stronghold unprotected. They know I haven't an army big enough to launch a full scale attack without risking leaving the castle unguarded," Varik exclaimed, slamming his hands down on the table.

"There are risks to this," Lorna warned. "Even with the passes for cover, they might find us out. And we do not know when my sister will march." Lorna pursed her lips, unsure.

"She marches," Arianette said, "already."

Varik and Lorna stared at her.

"How do you know?" Lorna asked, her voice shaky.

"I know." Arianette's expression was guarded.

Lorna looked uncertain as she studied Arianette with narrowed eyes.

But Varik set his chin and stabbed a red pin into the map in the center of the Valley of the Ancients.

"Let us begin, then," he said.

For a moment he looked wistful and everyone at the table knew what he was thinking. Varik Skyborn was thinking that he wished his brother, Braedin, was here to set the plan in motion.

Only Arianette knew that he was.

CHAPTER 36

THE VALLEY OF HEROES

The army of Sky could not travel by air for fear of being spotted by Ereda's forces, so they picked their way through rocky terrain, moving at what felt like a snail's pace. Every so often a gaggle of Accursed would attack. The mindless mobs were no real threat, but they further slowed their progress.

Upon reaching the series of narrow channels cut into the rock above the Valley of Heroes they set up camp. Overnight the weather turned, a storm not of Varik's making blew through the mountains.

Despair fell over the camps, and the day broke gray and bleak. The sun failed to rise, instead the misty drizzle that had begun the night before turned to a soaking rain as dawn broke. The dusty gray earth became a thick slippery mud. Ankles turned in the sucking mud. Man and beast wounded before the fighting had even begun.

Their pennants hung limp in the cold still air; the silver and blue for the Sky Court. No other banners. No other armies. Varik searched the sky for signs of the red and gold of Asheron and the Fire Fae, the lavender and turquoise of Nimione 's Sea Court, the rust and black of the Court of Earth.

All had abandoned the Skylord.

By the time the sun crested the mountain range, the war drums of the Shadow Fae had grown audible, rumbling like low thunder as they passed through the valley. The slow steady sound of their doom marching upon them. No one in the camps seemed confident of great glory to come in the battle ahead.

Varik, Lorna, and Arianette trudged through the mud on their silver winged stallions. No one, not even the Skylord, dared take to the skies, knowing the Shadow conjurors were so close at hand. Thus far, they had kept themselves hidden. Varik used the winds to conceal their scent and throw the Shadow Fae off their track. Their only advantage lay in the element of surprise. Ereda had the advantage in numbers and the Sky Fae, never a militant Court to begin with, had grown even more lax and undisciplined under years of Varik's neglectful rule.

They moved through the camps silently. Any attempt at rallying the troops felt a waste of precious energy that might be necessary to simply survive the day to come.

"The hour draws near," Lorna said.

On the horizon the black smoke of ruined villages steamed up into a slate hued sky. In the distance, Ereda's black pennants fluttered, streaming out for miles as they funneled into the valley. Only the bluffs they stood upon and Varik's Windsingers stood between the Sky Court and complete annihilation.

"I mislike this rain. It's an ill omen," Varik said grimly.

"Let me parlay with my sister," Lorna pleaded with the Skylord.

"We have nothing to offer for peace. I will never hand the Sky Court over to her, or Arianette, and she will settle for nothing less. Besides, she'll likely kill you if you try. And we can't have that. I made a geis to protect you from her," Varik said with a sad slow smile.

Arianette ignored them both, gazing dispassionately down at what might be her doom. She had painted her face in the swirling green war paint favored by the Elves and wore her hair wound in the high tight coils.

"Perhaps someone has figured out how to kill hope after all," Arianette said.

Just then a ray of sunshine cut through the thick cover of clouds. It streamed down, illuminating the desolate valley in white light.

But still there was no surge of hope in their chests.

CHAPTER 37

RENDEVOUS

Amidst the chaos of the preparations, Arianette's absence went unnoticed. She crawled along the narrow rock cuts, slinking through the shadows, until she reached the cave secreted away within the rocky crags of the mountain pass.

He was standing with his back to her when she approached the mouth, his majestic griffon wings folded at the shoulders. When the scent of her wafted in on the rapidly cooling evening air, Braedin turned to face Arianette. He smiled, almost shyly, conscious of the runes covering his body.

"What has she done to you?" Arianette asked, approaching. She traced her fingers along the raised silver scars that ringed Braedin's biceps, following their lines up his neck to the spiral rune centered on his forehead, twin to her own. His scars were a perfect mirror image of the pulsing runes etched into Arianette's flesh.

"Only the same as she's done to you," he said softly, stiffening at her touch.

Arianette shook her head slowly. In the failing evening light her profile looked severe.

"No. Muírgan didn't do this to me. This is who I am. This is who I've always been, deep inside."

She did not look at Braedin, instead running her eyes along the paintings on the cave walls. The whirls and swirls were all familiar to her now; the hieroglyphs of her mother's people. This clandestine cave was a holy Elven place.

Braedin drew up behind her. He placed his hand on her shoulder and turned her around to face him again. Arianette looked up at him with blazing eyes, her lips set in a hard thin line.

"Your geis with my brother?" he asked.

"I was soul-fasted to Varik during the Reckoning." Braedin's expression darkened, but Arianette went on. "I am bound to stand beside him and fight, and I shall."

"But when the time comes?" Braedin pressed. For just a moment Arianette's mask of stony composure slipped, but she quickly regained her stoic expression.

"When the time comes, I will do what needs to be done."

Braedin studied Arianette. He opened his mouth as if to say something, then closed it again.

Arianette levelled her gaze at him.

"I know, Braedin, you do not need to say it."

"What?" he looked startled.

"I know that you love me."

Arianette rose on her tiptoes and kissed him, hard and fast.

Then she gestured and shifted into the form of a pure white eagle.

With a piercing cry, she soared from the belly of the cave to face the war outside.

219

CHAPTER 38

MISSING IN ACTION

The low moaning war horns cut through the pounding of drums as Ereda's forces entered the valley at last. They spilled like ink across the landscape, a single massive shadow blotting out the horizon, Accursed driven forward by Shadow Conjurors mounted on Nightmares snorting flames. Into the lowlands they poured from the high steppes, fanning out like a wave crashing.

And now Arianette was gone.

"What do you mean *gone*?" Varik asked, incredulous. Mounted on a Pegasus with bells braided into its mane, he wore fighting leathers, not armor, his crystalline sword sheathed on his back, long hair silver bound.

Lorna fidgeted, fingering the runes around her wrists.

"I mean, she's gone. I've looked everywhere. No one saw her leave."

Varik cursed, torn between irritation and concern. It seemed unlikely that Ereda had gotten her hands on Arianette. If their cover was blown, the Shadow Empress would've made some surprise move against them, taken advantage of their vulnerability.

"She has been acting strange, Varik. Ever since you unbound her. You know that. Do you really know who she is and what she fights for? I can't say I do. I'm afraid she might have—"

Varik looked at Lorna sharply and she broke off.

"She is geis-bound, Lorna. She would not betray me. She is half Fae and knows her life would be forfeit," he growled.

"Perhaps her cause is more important to her than her life," Lorna muttered.

Varik shot her a black look.

"She will come back," he declared. But there was uncertainty in his voice that he could not hide.

5

Varik's forces were scattered throughout many small passes, but he visited each band of Windtalkers. He and Lorna swept through their ranks, offering words of encouragement and keeping their eyes open for signs of Arianette.

But Lorna was right. She was nowhere. She had, it seemed, vanished.

"We cannot wait much longer," Lorna said, biting her lip. "If we miss this opportunity, we may not have another."

Varik gazed down into the valley teeming with the decaying forms of the Accursed. Soon the bloodthirsty creatures would be beneath them, would scent them out, and would blow their cover, if they didn't act.

"We will have to fight without her." Varik's jaw muscles worked hard, his body was a live wire, knotted with tension.

The sun was slipping in and out of thick cloud cover, but at least the rain had stopped.

"Lorna, whatever happens here today," he began, studying her. She wore her black robes as always, black and gold hair secured away from her face in a multitude of tiny braids. "When this is done, I release you from your geis."

Lorna's violet eyes were wide and luminous. There was a spark behind them Varik had not expected to see there.

"I don't stand beside you because of our geis, or because I hate my sister, Varik. I stand beside you because I am your friend."

She jogged her stallion forward to peer over the edge of the ravine with him. Below, the Accursed were beginning to sniff the air, to sense the prey hidden all around them.

"So it is now, or never."

Varik whispered a word, commanded a breath of wind to send it to his captain's ears. Then he sent a prayer up to Xennia, raised his voice and cried:

"ah, Skyborn!"

There was a thunder of trumpets. His army broke from the passes. A flurry of arrows fell as the descended upon the undead army in the valley.

CHAPTER 39

THE HEAT OF BATTLE

At first it seemed there was hope, as Lorna had said. The Accursed were mindless and used no strategy in their attacks. Varik and his Windtalkers snatched the air from their lungs, conjured up cyclones that ripped them limb from limb. Lorna's shadows descended upon them, black voids that swallowed them whole by the dozen.

But the Accursed were only the beginning. Behind them loomed the Shadow Weavers.

Ereda rode at their head, a black staff topped with a gleaming orbs held aloft before her. As they approached, the hopelessness of the situation finally came crashing down upon Varik's army.

Streaks of black antimatter rained down on the forces of the Sky Court like dark stars, hissing with static as they fell from the sky. The Windtalkers' magic fizzled, ineffectual. The soldiers gazed in wonder and horror as their air shields broke. Their spells died in their mouths, choking them.

"What foul sorcery is this," Varik croaked, as his own spell work faltered. "Hold the line," he shouted to his crumbling flank.

Varik raised his hands skyward, struggling to call a storm. A swirling vortex of air sprang up around him just in time to deflect a shadow bolt. It smashed into the weakened shield so hard that it drove him backwards, sending him staggering straight into the path of another bolt.

Lorna appeared at his side shrieking as she dispersed the bolt of antimatter with black magic of her own.

"Varik, we have to fall back," she cried. "Ereda is using some kind of dampener on our magic."

Varik ground his teeth.

"I will not."

"If we stay here we die."

"We die either way," Varik said, breathing heavily and brushing his silvery hair from his brow. "I will not surrender to your sister." He slashed at an Accursed as it lumbered towards him. He severed its neck. It exploded into a shower of gray dust.

There was a sound like repeated explosions and the evening sky turned bright white around them. It stunned both armies and there was a lull in the fighting as they tried to determine what was happening.

Varik saw her first.

Arianette sat mounted on her ice white Unicorn wearing white armor leather, red hair streaming over her shoulders, an opal and emerald diadem set upon her brow. In her hand she held a standard emblazoned with the white wings emblem of the Court of Dreams against the backdrop of the Elven Heart of the Forest.

Around her, hundreds of Elves and solitary Fae had joined the fray. Where Varik's line was collapsing, Arianette's had reformed, driving Ereda's forces back towards the mouth of the valley. Whatever dampening spell Ereda had worked, the Elves and solitaries seemed unaffected by it.

They hurled their spells at the stunned Shadow Weavers, penetrating their shields, forcing them back away from the army of Sky.

"The Last Dreamer," Lorna, who had backed up to Varik, murmured.

"The Legion Queen," Varik corrected.

Then he snagged the reins of a stray Pegasus and hoisted himself onto its back.

"See the Legion Queen! The Queen from the Prophesy! The Queen who will reunite the realms, fighting beside you!" He strained his magic to amplify his words so that all of his army might hear him.

"HOLD YOUR LINE. Stand and fight!" the Skylord thundered.

More eyes shifted to Arianette. And the Sky Fae rallied, the ferocious power of hope buoying them.

Varik wasted no time.

He carried the momentum, hoisting his shimmering sword aloft despite the blood draining from his slashed forearm.

"Ah Skyborn!" he shouted and his men took up his rallying cry, surging forward again into the fray as the Elves cast their bark skin shields on the soldiers of Sky.

They mustered what wind they could and used it to strangle the lumbering forms of the Accursed, while Arianette and her Elves led the assault on the Shadow Weavers.

Arianette fought like a woman possessed, casting spells from every school of magic as she pushed through Ereda's line. The Shadow Empress had fallen back, but she would not escape. Arianette had made a geis with the Elven Queen for just this opportunity . Now she was twice -bound . Once to Varik, and once to Muírgan.

When she at last caught sight of Ereda again, all of her runes ignited at once. She felt as if she were being consumed by a firestorm of magic. The crowd was surging around her, but Arianette murmured a whispered word and a stream of pure blazing white light shot like a laser through the press of fighters.

She wanted to cover her ears, to block out the screams of the dying all around her. But she did not stop bearing down until she stood face to face with the Shadow Empress, Ereda Blackburn.

The woman who had destroyed her entire lineage, had forced her into a Mortal shell, had set all of this into motion.

"I will end you," Arianette shouted.

The shadow bolt gleamed as it shot out of Ereda's hand and soared through the air as if in slow motion.

But she hadn't aimed for Arianette.

The bolt was flying towards Varik.

Arianette screamed, taking to the sky on her white wings and hurling her body in front of the blade. Varik grabbed at her trying to throw her aside, screaming her name.

Too late.

The bolt struck Arianette dead center between her breasts. It collided with the rune. Painbringer flared. And suddenly the world around Arianette exploded into a shower of sparks and she heard a voice; a voice like her mother's. It sang that Elven melody that haunted her dreams.

She rose, red hair streaming amid the Wind Talker's gales, charred leathers singed away from her breast bone, runes covering her entire body. She was glowing, burning.

Then Arianette shrieked.

It was not a human scream. It was the other worldly cry that was the Elven war cry and it poured out of her until she had no breath left with which to scream.

Blood poured from the gaping hole in her chest, yet she stalked forward, feeling more alive than she had since the day that Veil had been sealed. The day she'd lost her mother, her father, her whole world.

The memory rushed back unbidden.

5

Amabella Gracelilly stood in the field beneath the Heart of the Forest, its broad branches bare above her head. Arianette's body was trussed and bound to the tree. Amabella's hand shook, her lips murmured the bittersweet song, the lament of the Elves, over and over.

Then she plunged the knife into Arianette's chest, binding her. Her mother had done this. Had bound her in a Mortal form.

Arianette, so young then, only a child, screamed as pain blossomed in her chest.

Her mother stopped singing and new voice joined hers as they began to chant.

Asheron Drogon.

"By the power of blood and flame we bind you. Mortal in Body, Elven in Spirit, Fae at Heart. Let these bonds hold until the time when the Legion Queen must rise."

5

Rage boiled up hot and black in Arianette's belly. The runes pulsed and throbbed. Her eyes rolled back in her head and turned bright crimson. She spread her wings and charged Ereda, one hand outstretched , the other pressed over her heart, over the pulsing bleeding rune.

Ereda threw up a shadow shield, but was too late. Vines sprang up from the ground, twisting and writhing, encircling the Shadow Empress' wrists and ankles. Great hooked thorns erupted from the vines, lashing out and embedding themselves in Ereda's flesh.

"Do not do this," Ereda howled. "You ally with the one who will end us all. You ally with Muírgan, who would burn the Courts. She will end you too, when she has no more need of you."

Ereda struggled at her bonds , but the vines held fast, only sinking their thorns deeper into her flesh , shredding her ruined black robes . Her blood was ashen gray as it streamed down her arms.

"I do not know," Arianette said "who will end me or what will become of the Courts. But your end comes now. By my hand."

Ereda stopped struggling. She straightened, lifting her chin higher.

"You are a broken thing. You believe ending me will fix you. But my blood cannot fill the emptiness in you. You stare into the Void, Arianette Gracelilly. Just as I do. Do not let it pull you in, or all is lost." Ereda's eyes were almost pitying.

The proud jut of her chin only made Arianette angrier. "Shut up. Say hello to the Void for me," she snarled.

Ereda opened her mouth to speak again, but Arianette waved a hand and the wind heeded her call. Invisible, silent, the strangling whip of the wind tore Ereda's words and life breath from her. She clutched at her throat as the air hissed out from her lungs.

Then Arianette gestured and bright white light leaked up from the ground in a miasma. Muírgan's skin peeled away in gray layers. Her bones seemed to liquefy, as if dipped in acid. There was a deep sucking noise as her body collapsed in on itself.

And then, in a single plume of grey matter, Ereda became one with the Void.

Arianette gazed at the place where the Shadow Empress has been. She felt nothing. No sorrow, no relief, no elation, no regret. She did not even feel pain, though blood still trickled from her wounds.

Around her, the gravity of what she'd done was becoming apparent on both sides of the fray. A collective cheer rose from the Sky Court's men at arms. The Shadow legions were laying down their arms, throwing their hands up in surrender, or taking to their heels, fleeing back towards the borders of the now leaderless Shadow Court.

The battlefield was all smoke and ash, blood, gore, singed corpses of Fae and Elf and Accursed alike. Braedin stood across the field from Arianette, his golden wings spread wide, his leather armor torn away from his chest where, just visible, pain-bringer was etched. One antler was shattered, and at his throat the Still Heart tattoo throbbed steady and blue.

Drenched in the blood of their enemies, streaked with gore like war paint, their tattooed bodies mirrored one another. Braedin's eyes flashed as their gazes met across the distance and Arianette felt trapped in the pressure, beneath the weight of his stare. It was the swansong of a kindred spirit calling to her.

With monumental effort she broke the connection, turning to glance up the hill towards where she had last seen Varik. He knelt in the earth, clutching the wounds on his face and chest. Wounds Arianette had caused when her magic had exploded. Lorna, unscathed, looking like the beautiful shadow reaper she was, crouched beside him, tending to him with her dark and powerful magic.

Lorna. It was Lorna's shoulder Varik had buried his face in. Not Arianette's. She looked up and offered Arianette a wistful smile, pulling Varik's body closer. Her dark eyes tracked from Arianette to Braedin and she nodded, as if in assent.

Arianette rose, stretched the tatters of her wings. She locked eyes with Braedin across the field again.

Then they both looked to Aciperre.

Aciperre raised his Elven iron sword high above his head. With a cry of:

"dryadalum docentur!" he charged towards the battered lines of the Sky Court army.

The army of Elves and Solitary Fae that Arianette had led obeyed his command. She did nothing to stop them as they turned their cloaks and charged towards the Sky Fae who had been celebrating their victory only moments before.

Take the Skylord and the Shadow Sorceress. Alive.

That was the command.

That had been the plan all along.

EPILOGUE

Lorna awoke with a start, her mind foggy and reeling. The stone was cold beneath her. Varik's eyes were upon her.

"I thought we had won the battle...?" his words dropped off as Lorna took his face in her hands, wiping a stray tear from his cheek.

"At least it is over and we are both still alive."

There was no triumph in her voice. The words rang hollow. Though the dungeon was silent, the crash of swords, the sizzle of magic, and the moans of the wounded still replayed in Lorna's mind. She could not seem to block them out, to focus on their current situation.

They had lost. But at what cost?

Had Arianette had gone over to the other side? Lorna had seen her flee to Braedin's embrace, and she knew she would have to tell Varik that. It broke her heart to do it, knowing he was already grieving for his men who lay dying on the gore drenched steppes.

"I saw her carried from the field. She might well be alive, just injured, and unable to get word—" Varik's head snapped up, his eyes narrowing.

"Who carried her from the field?" Varik asked, enunciating each word.

"Your brother. Braedin" Lorna said softly.

"If we ever escape from this dungeon... I will kill him."